SONG
OF THE
FAR
ISLES

NICHOLAS BOWLING

2 PALMER STREET, FROME, SOMERSET BA11 1DS

WWW.CHICKENHOUSEBOOKS.COM

Text © Nicholas Bowling 2021
Illustration © Olga Baumert 2021

First published in Great Britain in 2021
Chicken House
2 Palmer Street
Frome, Somerset BA11 1DS
United Kingdom
www.chickenhousebooks.com

Chicken House/Scholastic Ireland, 89E Lagan Road, Dublin Industrial Estate,
Glasnevin, Dublin D11 HP5F, Republic of Ireland

Cover and interior design by Steve Wells
Instrument illustrations by Nicholas Dowling
Typeset by Dorchester Typesetting Group Ltd
Printed and bound in Great Britain by CPI Group (UK) Ltd, Croydon, CR0 4YY

FSC
www.fsc.org
MIX
Paper from
responsible sources
FSC® C020471

1 3 5 7 9 10 8 6 4 2

British Library Cataloguing in Publication data available.

ISBN 978-1-912626-67-0
eISBN 978-1-913696-02-3

For Mary, Will and Andy

Also by Nicholas Bowling

Witchborn
In the Shadow of Heroes

THE FAR ISLES

The Tuning Rock

Great
Horn

Little
Horn

Little Drum

Tusk

Great Drum

The Spit

THE
GREAT
GULCH

Fiddlehead

THE ENDLESS SEA

The
Five
Fingers

Harp

NORTH

WEST

EAST

SOUTH

CITHARA

The cithara is the first of the instruments, and the most versatile. It is unique in not having a specific partner instrument, and will happily duet with any of the nine. Cithara players are just the same – open-minded, open-hearted and friendly to all (even when they should be more circumspect). Cithara players are creative, imaginative, and often characterized as dreamers. They usually have an adventurous streak, and have difficulty seeing the seriousness and danger of certain situations.

FIDDLE

Fiddle players have long had to endure the age-old joke about being 'too highly strung'. While it is true that they have a tendency towards worry, and do not cope well with change and disorder, they are also fiercely loving and selfless souls. They are tireless workers – often on the behalf of others – and their quick fingers make them exceptional craftsmen and women.

BARROW FIDDLE

Traditionally the accompaniment to funeral song. Players of the barrow fiddle are, like their instruments, a thoughtful and melancholy bunch. In general they are self-sufficient and happiest in their own company, but the friendships they do form are incredibly strong. To those who know them they are loyal, trustworthy and can always be relied upon for sound advice and a sympathetic ear.

SEAHORN

Brash and brassy, players of the seahorn are perhaps the most confident of musicians. They are born leaders. They love to be in the company of others, and others love to be around them – not least to catch their jokes and stories. Typically, seahorn players have inexhaustible amounts of energy, and are known to be spontaneous to the point of recklessness. Underestimate their mood swings at your peril . . .

BOMBARD

Bombard players are renowned for being deeply affectionate and soulful sorts (the bombard is often known by its colloquial name, 'the lover's pipe'). They want nothing more than to please other people, and the courtship of a bombardist can be a wearisome thing. They are, like fiddle players, very hard workers – although, unlike fiddle players, they are also impossibly disorganized. Always best to give a bombard player one task at a time.

REED PIPE

Reed pipers are often hard to pin down – never happy to settle in one place, or at one task, for too long. They have a reputation for being flighty, changeable and unreliable, but at the same time there is no one with quicker wits. Many a time has an overconfident seahorn player found themselves on the sharp end of a reed piper's tongue. And their feet are quicker still – with the smallest and lightest of the instruments, they are the best dancers on the Four Seas.

BAGPIPES

Bagpipers are some of the most gregarious musicians in the Far Isles – great talkers, great storytellers and (as the stereotype goes) great eaters and drinkers. Only cithara players can compete with their friendliness. They are known for their patience and compassion, and are nearly impossible to rouse to anger. On the rare occasions when they give in to their emotions, however, best set sail for another island . . .

BODHRÁN

The role of the drum is to hold a song together, so it is unsurprising that bodhrán players are the most steadfast and reliable of islanders. They say what they mean, and they mean what they say. A drummer is often called upon to settle disputes between more 'passionate' instruments – in fact, they can be so diplomatic and even-handed that they seem to lack any feelings at all. Do not be fooled by this. Under a bodhrán player's thick skin is a warm heart and a wicked sense of humour.

HANDPAN

The handpan is perhaps the oddest instrument in the Far Isles – somewhere between percussion and a tonal instrument – and handpan players are, without exception, eccentric folk. Their minds seem to work in ways that other musicians cannot fathom, which means they often befriend each other (or just talk to themselves). But beyond their outward strangeness they are fiercely intelligent, perceptive and imaginative. They often see solutions to problems where everyone else has failed.

1

Oran hauled hard on the mainsheet and brought her little boat around to face home. It was almost dark. The wind was blowing in the wrong direction now, forcing her to tack left and right over the swells. She could hear her cithara case colliding with the hull every time she turned. The waves were larger too, and slopped over the edges of the boat. Sometimes the prow would strike one of them head-on and send a blast of foaming, freezing seawater into her face. It felt good.

She looked behind her to see the sun inches from

the horizon. Tusk was well behind her. Ahead of her the sky was a thunderous blue, the same colour as her cithara, and on Little Drum people were starting to light lamps in their windows. Oran hoped one of them was her mother's. If she was at home, that meant she hadn't gone out looking for her.

The wind changed direction again, and she ducked under the boom as it swung around. She let the rigging play out through her fingers, which were pink and raw from practice. She didn't mind. It was a sign of a day well spent.

The boat scudded and dipped and again she heard her instrument thump against the wooden sides.

'Sorry,' she shouted over the snapping of the sail, 'but it's better to have you down there than risk you going overboard.'

The cithara seemed to go quiet after that.

She could see the harbour now and the flames of the lighthouse. Way above, on the clifftop, a farmer was herding her flock home with a reed pipe before the weather turned. The quayside was crowded with brightly coloured fishing boats, sloops, and a very handsome three-mast frigate. Oran wondered whose it was. Visitors from the Headland, it looked like, but they hardly ever came out this far.

The sun disappeared and the waves turned black. The thunder began like the purring of some great animal. Oran cursed and shivered. She'd been out in worse conditions than this, but her arms were getting tired from tacking back and forth, back and forth, and if she didn't get home quickly her mother's anger wouldn't be the worst of it. She'd be letting the whole island down.

The thunder cracked, urgently this time, and it started to rain. The wind still couldn't make up its mind where it wanted to go, but Oran wrestled the sail into position again and again and zigzagged her way to the harbour. The surface of the sea hissed, furred with raindrops, and the light of the lighthouse became a hazy orange globe. Everything else disappeared in the downpour. Before long there were three inches of water in the bottom of the boat, so she picked up her cithara and held it tightly in her lap.

'You'd better still be dry,' she muttered to the box. 'You owe it to me, remember? After your string snapped? Last week?'

As usual, the instrument didn't reply.

The boat limped into the harbour, carrying so much water it seemed moments from sinking. Oran leapt out and tied up the boat with a clumsy knot. The quayside was deserted apart from two or three ghasts whose forms shimmered in the pouring rain. That was one good thing about being dead, she thought. You never got wet.

'Good evening!' she said. She pushed a strand of wet hair out of her eyes. 'Well, not really, is it?'

They looked at her in surprise. No one else spoke to the ancestors like she did. The older folk thought her disrespectful, but she didn't care. She was happy to see them, and imagined they were glad to have a bit of conversation.

'Is Alick with you?'

They shook their heads slowly.

'Do you know where he is?'

'He may be in the Barrow,' said one, and his voice was like a gong, softly beaten.

'Oh well,' she said. 'I suppose I'll find him later. Whose is that swanky boat over there?' She gestured to the frigate, though it could hardly be seen through the pouring rain.

'Visitors,' said another. 'From the Headland.'

'We know not what they bring.'

'They came on an ill wind.'

Oran looked from one pale face to the next. 'Right-o,' she said. The ghasts were prone to these sorts of grave announcements. She never paid them much attention. 'Well, I'm not getting any drier out here. I should go and get ready for the dance. Nice talking to you all.'

She gave them a quick bow, and they bowed back, bemused.

Oran took the coastal path away from the harbour. On the top of the cliffs, the lamps still glowed in the windows of her parents' cottage. She knew her father would be experimenting with a pot of stew, and her mother would be fussing over the torcs or tuning her fiddle. Granny would be knitting the same blanket she'd been working on since Oran was born – it should have been ready for Oran's cot, but her grandmother had got carried away and now, fourteen winters later, she was still clickety-clacking away in her armchair.

Oran smiled and set off up the steep, slick path towards home.

She'd taken the cliff path thousands of times but still had to watch where she put her feet, particularly when it was dark and the weather was as bad as it was. She looked down rather than ahead, and halfway up the cliff she collided with something huge and immovable and soft around the edges. She lost her balance and nearly toppled over backwards. Two strong hands shot out and held her upright.

Oran peered through the rain. 'Oh,' she said. 'Hullo, Da.'

Her father was wearing his thick sealskin coat, whose pockets contained a variety of spoons and ladles and spatulas. His bagpipes were slung on his back.

'Oran!' he cried over the noise of the storm. 'Where on the Four Seas have you *been*?'

She shrugged. 'Practising,' she said, then added: 'You've got some food in your beard.' She tugged at his bristles.

'Practising? Where?'

'You know. Here and there.'

Her father narrowed his eyes. 'Let's see your hands,' he said.

She showed him her palms.

'Unless you've drastically changed your technique,' her father said, 'these are *not* the kinds of blisters you get from playing the cithara.'

'I just took a boat out for while . . .'

'You sailed to Tusk, didn't you?'

Oran didn't reply. She looked at her hands as though she'd never seen them before.

Her da sighed and ran his scarred fingers through his beard. 'Love, you know how dangerous that is! Sea's teeth, what is it about that old rock?'

'It's just quiet there,' she said. That was at least *half* true.

'You know how your maw feels about you sailing on your own, especially when the weather's like this.' The lightning lit them both for a moment, and was followed by a grumble of thunder. 'Listen to that! If you'd been any later you'd be on the seabed by now, and I'd have a ghast for a daughter.'

'Sorry,' she said.

'Tell that to your maw,' he said.

'She doesn't need to know, does she?'

'She knows you're late, that's for sure. That's why she sent me down here.'

'We've got ages, haven't we? If she's still at home—'

'She's not at home. Granny's at home. Your mother went ahead to the Broken Bottle an hour ago.'

'An hour ago? Why?'

Her da looked grim. 'Because that was when the dance started. You're meant to be on stage right now, Oran.'

≋2≋

The Broken Bottle was aptly named. The tavern was – against all odds – the oldest on the island, but after hundreds of years of misfortune hardly anything of the original building remained. From where Oran was standing, it looked like five or six different buildings thrown together in a heap. Parts were wooden, parts were stone. The roof bowed in the middle, and there was a turret inexplicably projecting from the southern end. The windows were all wildly different heights, pouring light and noise out on to the puddles in the town square.

The story went that it had originally been called simply 'The Bottle', but whoever had built the place had woven disaster into its very timbers. Even in Oran's lifetime, the tavern had suffered three fires, had twice lost its roof to the winds, had been crushed by a falling fir tree, and had collapsed at one end due to a particularly industrious family of moles who had taken up residence beneath it. But the people of Little Drum always came together to rebuild the place, and it had long since become an emblem of their hardiness and optimism. There were other taverns that were cleaner, brighter, that served better food and more sophisticated selections of whisky, but none of them were held in as much affection as the Broken Bottle.

And nowhere, not on Little Drum, or Great Drum, or the Five Fingers could you find better or louder songs.

From outside Oran could hear that things were, indeed, well underway. 'The Lover's Leap', it sounded like. The islanders were stomping and singing and joining in on their instruments, and her cithara had already started to hum on her back. Oran looked at her da and he raised his enormous eyebrows. She swallowed. She was very late.

She followed him through the open door and was struck with a wave of noise and sweat and steam.

These days Oran had to stoop under the crooked doorframe to get in – her maw had always said her daughter had the long, thin fingers of a cithara player, but now her arms and legs were following suit. She was already taller than all of the boys and girls her age, and her growth spurt showed no signs of stopping.

She left her da and made her way to the stage, laughing as she manoeuvred around the dancers, their faces red and gleaming from too much wine and too much leaping. Some of them stopped and pointed at her, others applauded and clapped sweaty hands on her shoulder. There were ghasts too, loitering in the tavern's few dark corners, who smiled and inclined their silver heads.

Oran always did her best to restrain her pride, because she knew it wasn't good for her soul or for her playing, but her heart was ready to burst. They were all there for her, she knew.

'You decided to come then, did you?'

Her mother popped up in front of her, thrusting the bow of her fiddle under Oran's nose.

Oran did her best sheepish grin. 'Hullo, Maw,' she said.

'Don't "hullo Maw" me, young lady! Where've you been? Off daydreaming no doubt. Talking to the sea cows!'

Oran didn't reply. Better that her mother thought

she had been away with the sea cows than sailing over the stormy sea to Tusk. She hadn't told her about Bard, either. How could she even begin to explain about Bard?

'You need to start thinking straight, girl. You're not a child any more. You got responsibilities.'

'I'm here, aren't I?'

'You're over an hour late! Just because you happen to be the best player on the island doesn't mean you can swan in here whenever you want.'

'But—'

'And just because these folk will wait to hear you play, doesn't mean they *should* wait. You got to respect your audience, Oran, no matter how good you are.' Her mother glared at her with her fierce, sea-grey eyes. 'Now,' she said, putting her fiddle on the bar, 'give your maw a hug.'

She squeezed Oran so tightly that the rainwater seeped out of her daughter's cloak on to the floorboards like she was a giant sponge. Oran squeezed back. She wished Maw worried less. It made Oran behave strangely – it made her want to disobey her parents *more*, and yet at the same time made her feel *worse* for disobeying them. She knew she was doing it out of love, but she couldn't quite say how this figured.

When her mother released her, she was smiling again.

'Now, then,' she said, 'have you thought about what we're going to play?'

In all honesty, Oran hadn't given it any thought. That was what people said was special about her. She played *unthinkingly*. Never needed to rehearse. Never needed to read the music. Could pick up a tune and turn it into something that brought tears to the eyes before she'd even heard the whole thing once through. Only Bard knew how to find and train that part of her intuition.

'What about,' she said, '"The Red Duchess"?'

'"The Red Duchess"! Absolutely not. I can't believe you even *know* that song. At your age!'

'But they'll love it, Maw!'

'They're drunk enough to love anything, Oran,' said her maw. 'Songs like that will get you into trouble. Besides, it's new. The ghasts won't thank you for it.'

'Maybe "Three Merry Widows"?'

'A bit tame.'

Not the way Oran played it, it wasn't.

'"The Sea Cow's Daughter"?'

'Aye, that's good. A good old song. We'll have a bit of fun with that.'

Oran's mother picked up her fiddle and they moved away from the bar towards the stage. The air was like warm soup, and within it there were strange odours that moved in complex currents and eddies. As Oran climbed the steps, the room erupted into applause, accompanied with hoots and stamps and little musical flourishes. Oran grinned and stared out at the packed tavern. The crowd looked on with pink, expectant faces, their birth instruments held aloft or clutched to their chests – fiddles, drums, reed pipes, bagpipes, seahorns, citharas and more.

She set the case of her own instrument on her lap and opened the clasps.

The frame of her cithara was like a crescent of autumn sky. The lacquer was a deep blue, inlaid with a curling detail of golden leaves. As was tradition, it was the ghasts who had chosen which instrument she should play. But the cithara itself had been made by both her parents while she was in her maw's belly, and she loved it like she loved them.

She lifted it carefully from the torc-wool lining. It was dry, even after it had been caught in the storm. She polished its frame roughly with a cloth, more out of ritual than necessity, and began to tune its seven strings. The audience began to settle as she made minute adjustments to the pegs, her eyes closed, waiting for that indescribable feeling of rightness as each string settled into its pitch alongside its fellows.

When she opened her eyes, the room was bright-eyed and silent. Her mother looked at her and gave a wry smile, as if to say: *I know you're enjoying this, but don't enjoy it too much.*

Oran adjusted the cithara on top of her thighs, cracked her long fingers and shaped the first chord.

> *When the world was young and the sea was new*
> *A man sailed oot wit' his lady true*
> *The fairest maid loved this fine laird:*
> *A sea coo blessed wi' a seaweed beard.*

Her mother had been right, though Oran didn't like to admit it. 'The Sea Cow's Daughter' went down a storm. The ghasts loved it, drifting out from the dark nooks of the tavern to whirl in amongst their descendants. They didn't look silver and hazy, like they usually did. The music made them blaze gold. They looked more *there*, more alive even than those who hadn't yet passed on.

Oran played and grinned, improvising snatches of new harmony and melody that made the whole room roar with surprise. There was no feeling like it. She looked at her maw, and her maw rolled her eyes.

The song twisted and turned through some twenty verses. There were hundreds in total, because different singers kept adding their own parts to the tale, but no one knew them all. Well, maybe Bard did. She seemed to know every song under the sun. The heart of the story followed the fisherman who fell in love with a sea cow. They had a daughter, who lived both above and below water. Oran loved it. She liked to think there was something of the sea cow's daughter in her, a girl of both the sea and the land. A girl who was a little different.

She finished her final verse and the dancers collapsed into their chairs, laughing and clapping. The ghasts beamed, outshining the blubber lamps. Oran looked to see if her friend Alick was among them. He wasn't there. That was fine. Alick played the barrow fiddle, and barrow fiddle players were notoriously antisocial.

'Another!' shouted someone in the crowd, though she couldn't see who.

The rest stomped their feet in approval. Oran looked at her maw again. Her face was red and pouring with sweat from keeping pace with her daughter. She gestured with her bow.

'If you've got it in you, my love,' she said. 'I'll have to sit this one out.'

'"The Red Duchess"!'

Another whoop of approval. Her mother shook her head. Oran turned back to her audience and smiled. She began to play it anyway.

She didn't know why Maw worried so much. Little Drum was so far removed from the Headland that the Court, the Duke and the Duchess were just the stuff of stories. They were a good way to get weans to behave. If you didn't, the Red Duchess would come for you . . .

Hark to the song of the Red Duchess
The fount of all the seas' distress;
A cruel and murdering fiend, no less,
Her crimes too many to confess!

Oran was halfway through the song when she realized that the room had gone quiet. She looked up from her instrument, her fingers still finding their own way through the tune. The ghasts had withdrawn into the shadows, and the rest of the islanders were mute. Her mother's face had turned from red to white.

The door to the Broken Bottle was wide open and still quivering on its hinges. There was a tall, slim woman standing just inside, wearing a black dress bound in tight hoops of whalebone. She looked as though she had just come from a funeral. Her hair was scraped backwards and clasped out of sight, so her head was a perfect white oval: an egg balanced on a candlestick.

Next to her was a tiny man holding an umbrella. He was wearing enormous heels but still had to stand on tiptoes to protect the woman's head from the rain. In fact, Oran would have sworn he was a child, were it not for the circular goatee beard in the middle of his circular face. He wore the distinctive pantaloons of the Headland, and over one shoulder a sash with a red and black family skein she didn't recognize.

But the strangest thing was this: neither of them was carrying their birth instrument. She'd heard that Headlanders did not play as much music as the islanders, but this was astonishing to see. They may as well have walked in completely naked.

The man and woman were followed by a handful of guards in matching sashes and pantaloons and feathered caps, and finally by the island's mayors, a husband and wife. They fanned out through the tavern. Oran looked at her maw. Her maw was glowering at her.

The tiny man stepped forward and cleared his throat. 'Her Grace,' he said, 'Duchess Samhair of the Headland, and of the Near and Far Isles.'

The silence that followed made Oran's ears ache. She clutched her cithara so hard she thought she might break it. The stories were true, then. She'd misbehaved, and the Red Duchess had come for her.

3

The woman moved stiffly among the scattered tables of the Broken Bottle, followed by her assistant and the two mayors. She gave suspicious, or perhaps fearful, glances to the ghasts. Did they have ghasts on the Headland? Oran didn't know.

A murmur passed through the tavern. The too-loud scrape of a chair on the floorboards. The drip, drip, drip of the leaking roof. The Duchess lifted her skirts and came up on to the stage, where she stood between Oran and her maw, ignoring both of them. The mayors stood awkwardly to one side.

Oran looked the woman up and down and tried to convince herself there had been some mistake. It *couldn't* have been the Red Duchess. She looked nothing like the woman from the song. Her hands weren't bloodstained, her eyes didn't blaze like hot coals. In fact, nothing about her was red, apart from a small patch of her family skein pinned to the front of her dress.

'Have they finished?' the Duchess said to her hanger-on.

'Yes, Your Grace.'

She bent a little closer to him, as though she hadn't heard.

'*Yes, Your Grace,*' he said, louder. 'Not a note.'

Oran frowned. She watched the Duchess put her hands to her ears and pluck out a pair of bejewelled earplugs. The Duchess handed them to the little man, who cleaned them discreetly with a black and red handkerchief and put them in an oyster shell.

'Good evening,' she said to the room, sounding as if she wished them anything but. Her voice was lower than Oran had been expecting. She could have sung bass in the fisherwomen's choir. 'It would normally be my custom to address you formally in your town hall, but since, apparently, you have no town hall . . .'

That wasn't strictly true. They had a hall, but it was currently being used to store apples and pears and root vegetables in readiness for the Festival of First Fruits.

'Your mayors suggested I speak to you here' – she gave an uncomplimentary look to the bare rafters of the tavern – 'since it is such a popular occasion. So. Here I am. And here you all are.'

There was a nervous wheeze from somebody's bagpipes.

'To begin, I would like to apologize for my absence since the tragedy last year at the Court.' She paused and looked out at the crowd, as if challenging someone to give voice to the rumours about how, exactly, that tragedy had come to pass. 'I am aware that no Duke or Duchess has come to visit the Far Isles in decades, and were it not for events at home I would have visited my tenants a good deal earlier.'

Oran frowned. Tenants? What did she mean by that?

'Unfortunately, the loss of so many members of the royal family threw the Headland into no little chaos, and a tour of the islands was out of the question. Now the Headland is settled, though, so I have been able to venture further abroad, and for the past several weeks I have been giving the Near and Far Isles the attention they deserve. How sad that Little Drum should be the last destination on my itinerary.' And then she turned and fixed Oran with a stare and Oran saw that, yes, her eyes *were* coals: bright, blue coals that left you frostbitten. 'I fear,' she said, 'it should have been my first.'

There was a long pause. The Duchess's gaze never faltered, and Oran was forced to look at her feet. Had the Duchess heard the song, or hadn't she? There was more anxious muttering from the patrons of the tavern. People laid gentle hands on their instruments to calm them. One of the mayors coughed.

'It is our honour and our, um, pleasure, to have you as our guest,' said the husband. He was a portly man who played the bombard. He fiddled with the valves of his instrument as he spoke. 'Perhaps you would join us for tonight's dance? I mean, you don't have to, um, dance. You can just listen. If you would like. Oran here is our most talented singer and musician, perhaps, she could, um, compose something for you here and now. Something to, um, commemorate this, um, wonderful . . .'

The mayor trailed off. Oran could feel her cithara protesting in her lap, a low vibration from the depths of its hollow body.

'A song would be most inapt,' said the Duchess. The little man was trying and failing to suppress a smile. She turned back to the room. 'As well as wanting to apologize, I have come to inform you of several new laws that have been passed through Court since

I inherited the Duchy last year. Firstly, regarding kelp.'

There were bemused looks around the tavern. Some even smiled. Surely the Duchess hadn't come all this way to discuss the price of seaweed?

'There is a glut of kelp and kelp-based products on the Headland. We are therefore limiting the import of kelp to a maximum of one hundred tons per boat per week. I hope this does not prove too much of an inconvenience.'

There were a few barely suppressed chuckles. That might have made a difference to merchants on the east of the Headland, where huge trawlers scoured the seabed clean, but out here a kelp farmer would be happy to accrue a hundred tons in a whole year.

'Secondly. The Opera are still at large and sailing among these isles. Whilst it has always been our strong recommendation that you do not invite them into your harbours, it is now forbidden by law. I hope you will agree that this is a necessary step to protect your homes and loved ones.'

That was met with a mixed response. Some islanders loved the Opera and their wild perform-ances. Others thought they were little more than musically inclined pirates. While the audience was digesting this, the Duchess quickly made her final statement.

'Thirdly, and most importantly, is the Bill of Quietude. Effective immediately, my men will be enforcing the cessation of all musical activities, and the confiscation of all musical instruments.'

It took the room a few moments to make sense of what she had said. It was like being rolled in a rough swell – darkness, silence, a suffocating weight, then rising to the surface where all was noise and thrashing foam.

The tavern erupted. The islanders got to their feet, shouting and stamping and beating their drums in fury. Some got out of their chairs and surged towards the front of the stage. Some were laughing out loud. The absurdity of it!

'By the Chorus, this ain't the Headland here!'

'The only way you'll get my fiddle is by taking it from my *dead fingers*!'

'It's our life, you bottom-feeding fool! Our whole *life*!'

The Duchess stood and weathered these cries, a stack of granite in a rough sea. She didn't move or speak. One of her eyes fluttered slightly, as though she was suffering from a migraine. Oran's fingers twitched restlessly on the strings of her instrument. She wanted to start playing again. Or rather her instrument did. There wasn't really any difference.

Eventually it was the mayor and mayoress who

brought the tavern under control, seeing that a riot was not the best way to argue their case.

'Your Grace,' said the mayor, once the noise had subsided, 'as you have heard, we cannot give up our instruments, much less our music. May I ask, um, why such a law has been passed?'

The Duchess frowned for a moment, then gestured around the Broken Bottle. 'Really? I mean, *look* at you all.'

The man with the umbrella laughed, and the room descended into chaos again.

'Perhaps,' said the mayoress, raising her voice above the din, 'you could be more specific?'

Again the Duchess waited for the storm to die down. 'Thankfully my ears were stopped when I arrived. But I know intoxication when I see it. It's been the same on all the islands. The same picture of . . .' She searched for the word. '*Dissolution*. Loose tongues and loose morals. This is what singing encourages.'

'Oh, rotgut!' said the mayoress.

The Duchess gave another one of her blistering stares. 'Indeed? I know the kinds of songs you sing out here. I have not heard them personally, nor do I want to. But Lord Magmalley here is kind enough to give me the gist.'

'They're just silliness, Your Grace,' the mayor said.

'Remind me of the line, Magmalley. Something about murdering my own parents and feeding them to the lugworms?'

Oran knew the exact verse of 'The Red Duchess' she was referring to. She could feel her maw's eyes upon her from the other side of the stage.

'I believe it mentioned something of that sort,' said Magmalley. 'It brings tears to my eyes even now, Your Grace.'

'This is not silliness,' said the Duchess. 'This is treason.'

The mayors clutched their instruments to their chests, he his bombard, she her seahorn. Oran watched the mayoress take several deep breaths to compose herself, then approach the Duchess with her head held high.

'I will be the first to apologize, Your Grace, if you have been offended by this shanty, or that ballad. But that is no reason to deprive the islands of music in its entirety. We have a saying here: you are taking a harpoon to fish for minnows.'

'Then let me explain in terms you can understand,' said the Duchess. 'Songs are, indeed, like fish. Slippery things. You think you have caught one, and then it turns up in a bay on the next island along. My dear, I am simply spreading my nets wide enough to ensure that none escape.'

'But our music is everything to us. *Everything*. It is the very air that we breathe, out here.'

'Nonsense,' the Duchess said. 'I've never seen a man die for lack of music.'

'But you see, Your Grace,' said the mayoress, quivering with rage, 'that *is* what will happen if you take it away from us. Music is the very heart of our community. It is what defines us, together and as individuals, living and dead. Song is our identity. Our history. Our memory.' More yelling from the islanders, but she spoke over the top of them. 'Without our songs we have no connection with our past. If you take away our music, you will take away our ancestors with it.'

Oran wasn't sure what the mayoress meant by that. She looked around at the ghasts. They simmered, blue and sullen, on the fringes of the hall. She thought of Alick again. Where was he?

'I would suggest,' said the Duchess, 'that you focus more on the *future* than the past. The Headland has been without music for only a few months and the progress we have made has been very pleasing. It's time you joined civilization, I think.'

'And if we refuse?'

'You will be evicted.'

The islanders could bear it no longer. They stood up, jeering and swearing and playing wild flourishes on their instruments. Oran listened hard. Her cithara growled with dissatisfaction in her hands.

The Duchess winced to hear the islanders' instruments and snapped her fingers at Lord Magmalley. He opened the oyster shell and handed over her ornate earplugs.

'You may play and sing to your heart's content tonight,' she said, though nobody could hear her. 'Tomorrow Lord Magmalley and his men will begin their collections.'

In went the earplugs, and she made a sign to her guards. They made a tight cordon around her and escorted her out of the seething tavern. The tip of Magmalley's umbrella was the only thing that showed he had gone with them.

'**Y**ou had to play it, didn't you?'

Oran's maw came storming across the stage, wielding her bow like a cutlass.

'What?' said Oran.

'"The Red Duchess"!'

'I didn't know she was going to just walk through the door, did I?'

'I *told* you not to.'

'I don't think she heard me.'

''Course she heard you. And if she didn't, little lord what's-his-name did.'

Oran let her maw march around until she'd worked off some steam. 'But we can change her mind, can't we?' she said.

'You saw her, Oran. Did she look like a woman who's easily persuaded?'

'I'm sure we can. If there's a song that's made her angry, there's a song that can calm her down. What is it that Granny always says? *Song for winter, song for spring, song for sorrow*, something, something . . .'

'I wish I had your optimism, my girl.' Her maw looked at Oran sadly. 'I wouldn't be surprised if she made a special example of you, after that performance of yours.'

They were interrupted by Oran's da, who had shouldered his way through the crowd and was standing at the front of the stage. He was still in his thick coat, mopping his red and shining brow with a handkerchief.

'What's happened here?' he said. 'Who was that I just saw leaving?'

Oran and her maw looked at each other.

'Weren't you here?' said Oran.

'I nipped out to check on Granny,' he said. 'Just got back. Why's everyone looking so furious?' He looked at Oran. 'You didn't play the one about the sea cucumber again, did you?'

They climbed down from the stage to join him.

Oran's maw told him what had happened and her da's huge eyebrows collapsed towards his nose.

'The Duchess? That was her?' He pointed at the door.

Oran nodded.

'But she can't do that, can she?' he said. 'I mean, practically speaking.'

'Of course she can!' cried her maw. 'She's the Duchess! She can do whatever she likes!'

Her da hefted his eyebrows back up to the top of his head. 'Well, I'm sure we can change her mind,' he said. 'Get Oran to play her something from her repertoire. Like Granny says. *Song for winter, song for spring, song for beggars*, something, something.'

Oran lit up. 'See!' she cried. Of course a bit of music could help. Music could do anything. If there was one thing she'd learnt from Bard, it was that. It was just a matter of finding the right tune, the right words to match it.

Her maw sighed with exasperation. 'Oran has already sung one too many songs tonight,' she said.

'That's why I should be the one to put it right!' said Oran. 'Why don't I go to her ship now? I could catch her before she leaves.'

'You? By yourself?'

'Yes.'

'By the Chorus, you are full of yourself, young lady!'

'Please?'

'Out of the question, Oran!'

'Why not?'

'Firstly, no one's doing anything until the ghasts tell us to.'

'But—'

'And secondly, earplugs or no, the Duchess is not going to listen to a wean.'

'Aha!' said Oran, victorious. 'I thought you said I wasn't a child any more? I thought you said I had responsibilities? Well, I'm taking on a responsibility now, aren't I?'

Her maw was saved from having to answer that by the mayors. They took to the stage and played several long notes in unison to calm the sea of voices and instruments. The tavern fell silent again. Her maw turned to listen, and Oran felt she'd had her victory cruelly snatched from her.

'I think,' said the husband, 'that we should, um, postpone the dance for another time. The ghasts have called a Moot to discuss this, um, unprecedented situation. In the meantime, I suggest you go to your homes and sing your hearth songs, and when tomorrow comes, well, um, perhaps—'

His wife cut in. 'When tomorrow comes,' she said, 'you lock your doors.'

Oran fidgeted with the tuning pegs on her cithara.

The island never did anything without a Moot. The mayors couldn't even decide what colour bunting to put up without referring it to the ghasts for discussion. Such meetings could last for days. Letting everyone who had ever lived and died on Little Drum have their say took a long time. The Duchess would no doubt be long gone by the time they finally reached a decision.

'Can *I* go to the Moot?' she asked her maw.

'Absolutely not! You know you're not allowed in the Great Barrow.'

'Da, can I go to the—?'

Her maw cut her off. 'Oran! Leave it! You're coming home with us, and we'll have a good sing while we wait for the ghasts to think of a way out of this.'

Oran chewed her lip. She'd have to get the ghasts on her side. Luckily there was someone she knew who could help with that.

She set her instrument back in its case and snapped the clasps closed and slung it on to one shoulder.

'Excuse me,' said her maw. 'Where do you think you're going?'

'For a swim.'

Her maw looked suspicious. 'A swim?' she said. 'Right now?'

'A quick one. In the Tears. Just to clear the old head.'

'But—'

'I'll come back to play with you all later.'

'Oran—'

But Oran was already on her way out of the door.

The storm had passed and the moon was out. Oran took the coastal path that wound along the cliffs above the harbour. Below, she could see the Duchess's guards wandering about the quayside, and her slender boat, its bright red sails illuminated by the lamps on deck.

The path was sodden and the puddles shimmered like quicksilver. Her route took her over the meadows, past the great flocks of sleeping torcs, down to the kelp farms on the eastern side of the island. Beyond the great racks of salty, stinking weed, the path forked and she made her way down to the Tears.

Concealed from the great Endless Sea to the west, the Tears was a perfectly circular lagoon that filled at high tide. Great cliffs of granite towered over the water, carved into strangely geometric shapes, like brickwork. Every edge and surface of these enormous blocks was carpeted with thick green moss. From the top of the cliffs tumbled a waterfall, which fell from such a height it turned to mist before it hit the surface of the lagoon. In the moonlight it was a pale and glittering rainbow.

The stories said that this was where Dunhaidh had landed after making the first crossing from the Headland, many hundreds of years ago. Along the way his wife had fallen from his ship and the first thing he did on arrival was to weep and sing for his lost love, and his tears had filled the pool. Oran thought the name far too mournful. She loved it here. The only thing that made her happier than swimming in the Tears was playing her cithara. It was also Alick's favourite place to think, and thinking was what he spent most of his days and nights doing.

She couldn't see Alick when she reached the end of the path. She checked all his usual haunts: the cave under the falls, the rotten, upturned boat, the rock that looked like a giant snail. No sign of him.

'Alick?' she whispered. Even when she spoke under her breath her voice was amplified and echoed back at her by the amphitheatre of rock. 'Are you here?'

There was no reply. Perhaps he had heard about the Moot. Ghasts had ways of communicating that Oran didn't understand. Perhaps he had already returned to the Great Barrow.

She looked out over the lagoon and saw a tremble in the surface, a quivering brightness like the moon's reflection, though the moon was behind her, and the brightness seemed to hover a few feet above the water.

She walked into the pool up to her calves. 'Alick?' she called. 'Is that you?'

'There's a wispfish in there.'

Oran squawked in surprise, tripped over, cut her knee on a rock, then scrambled back from the water's edge.

'Alick, *please* stop doing that.'

She peered out from behind the boulder and saw him standing on the shore, his pale, delicate features distorted in a frown.

'I thought you should know.'

'Thank you, but I wish you wouldn't just . . . pop up like that.'

'Oh. Yes. Sorry.'

Alick should have been the same age as Oran, but he had fallen overboard on a fishing trip when he was nine years old. His was the only body they'd been able to find, and the only one of his family given the proper rites. As a ghast he would never look or sound any older than his nine living years, but he spoke with the seriousness and world-weariness of a man who had lived too long and seen too much.

'How long have you been there?' Oran asked.

'This whole time.'

'What were you doing?'

'Thinking.'

'You didn't think to say hello?'

'I'm a little preoccupied, Oran.'

He was always preoccupied with something or other.

Oran stared out at the mirrored surface of the lagoon. The second moon was still there, bobbing a few feet above the water.

'A wispfish, you say?'

'Aye.'

'I thought they lived in deeper waters than this.'

'This one must have been washed in by the tide.'

The hovering lantern suddenly went out.

'Well. Thank you for telling me.'

'You're welcome.' He counted on his fingers. 'I make that . . . twenty-two.'

'It is *never* twenty-two. It's about fifteen.'

The exact tally of how many times Alick had saved Oran's life was a constant bone of contention. Alick joked, in his gloomy way, that it was completely unfair that out of the two of them *he* was the ghast and she was the one who was still flesh and blood. He'd been her advisor, her lookout, her voice of reason for as long as Oran could remember. If there were treacherous currents, chossy rocks, or bad-tempered squids to be avoided, Alick was always the one to spot them.

'Why did you come here, Oran?' he asked.

'I came to talk to you.'

'About the Duchess?'

'Yes.' She paused. 'How do you know about that?'

'I was there.'

'Where?'

'Up in the roof.'

'Why were you in the roof?'

'Quieter up there.'

'Oh.'

Oran twiddled her thumbs. She loved Alick inside and out, but there were times when the difference between them seemed particularly marked; that death had set a gulf between them that couldn't always be crossed.

'You realize how serious this is, don't you?' he said. 'This could be it. For me. For all the ghasts.'

'Oh Alick. Don't be so melodramatic. Ghasts don't just disappear.'

'Didn't you hear what the mayoress said?'

'I did, but I thought that was . . . I don't know. A figure of speech.'

'No songs, no ghasts, Oran. It's that simple. If the Duchess gets her way, then it's the Long Silence for all of us.'

'But if you go, then who'll tell us when to sow the crops?'

He shrugged.

'Who'll tell us about the tides?'

Again he didn't reply. Oran began to feel the tickle of panic.

'Who'll teach us new songs? Where will Da get his new recipes from? We can't just work all these things out in our *heads*, can we?'

'I don't know what the answer is,' he said. 'I suspect there isn't one. The older ghasts have been saying this will happen for years. The Silence. It's like they've always known it was coming.'

Oran's cithara was making a troubled humming on her back.

'There has to be an answer. We'll have to change the Duchess's mind.'

'And how will we do that?'

'I'll sing something for her.'

'You think nobody else in the Far Isles has considered that?'

'Maybe. But nobody else in the Far Isles can play as well as me.'

She heard her maw tutting from several miles away. But it was true.

'I don't think that is a good idea,' said Alick. His favourite eight words.

'Why not?'

'You're being daft. Think about it, Oran. Why would she listen to a song if she hates music so much?'

'She just needs to hear the right one.'

He shook his head. 'Your logic is flawed. Besides, the Moot is still in session. You can't just run off to her ship and claim you represent the whole island. You could make things a whole lot worse, Oran. I know you don't mind disobeying your maw, but even *you* wouldn't go against the ghasts, and they haven't made you their spokeswoman.'

'Well,' said Oran. She scratched her ear. 'Yes. Right. That is why I came to talk to you in the first place.'

'What do you mean?'

'I need you to go and put my name forward. Tell them that I'll sing.'

'I don't hold much sway in the Great Barrow, Oran. Look at me. I'm hardly what you'd call an elder.'

'But everyone gets to speak at the Moot, don't they? That's the point of a Moot.'

'Yes, but—'

'Then just say a little bit on my behalf.'

'Even if they agree, what are you going to sing for her? How are you going to choose the perfect song for a woman who hates music and everything about it?'

'I'll ask Bard.'

His face went transparent with worry. 'You know my thoughts on Bard.'

'You've never even met her.'

'I *can't* meet her,' he protested. 'Ghosts have to stay on the island.'

'Only in theory. I'm very happy to take your ashes with me next time.'

'No thank you. Even if I could come, I've had quite enough of seafaring for one lifetime.'

'Suit yourself.'

He looked at her closely. She could see the outlines of the rocks through him, as if his face was a grimy window.

'I wish you'd be more careful, Oran. You don't know anything about her.'

'I know this much,' she said, getting to her feet, 'She is the most wonderful singer, and most wonderful teacher, I have ever met. And you would agree, if you'd just accompany me one day.'

'Not a chance.'

'Then trust me.'

'I'd like to, Oran, but . . .' He looked at her seriously. 'It sounds like there's something strange about her.'

'Well, that's probably why we get on, isn't it?' said Oran. 'Now, go to the Moot and say your bit. Remember to tell them about my new thirteen-note scale. That'll make *anyone* sit up and listen.'

She tried to hug him, but as usual he slipped

through her grasp and she ended up kissing her own forearms.

'Sorry,' she said. 'Force of habit.'

Then she skipped home, already excited at the thought of returning to Tusk.

⟫5⟪

The following morning, Oran was awake before her parents and her grandmother. Sunlight the colour of new whisky shone through the gap beneath her curtains. A clear day. A good day for sailing.

She got up and threw on her skein, then tiptoed to the kitchen and took a heel of bread and half a cold sausage for her breakfast. On her way back she peered into her parents' tiny bedroom. They were asleep, their instruments hung above the headboard. They'd come home from the Broken Bottle after she'd returned from the Tears, both of them a little worse for wear, and now they seemed to be competing to out-snore each other. She thought about leaving them a note, but decided it was better to say nothing at all than to lie, especially when that lie was written in black and white.

She went to her bedroom, shouldered her cithara, and undid the latch on the front door.

'Off to Tusk, are you, love?' said her granny.

Oran leapt up and banged her head on the door-frame. She had to bite the inside of her cheeks to stop herself crying out.

Granny was sitting in the corner of the cottage in her favourite chair, her endless blanket spread over her knees. Her cithara was leant against the hearth, covered in a thin film of dust. Oran had never heard her play it. Sometimes she had spied through the cottage windows and seen her granny take it in her hands and examine it as if she had no idea how it worked. It was such a sad, strange thing.

'Please,' Oran whispered. 'Don't tell Maw and Da.'

'Who is he, then?' said her grandmother, not even trying to keep her voice down. 'Some handsome young piper?'

'What do you mean?'

'I'd say Tusk is the perfect spot for young lovers.' Granny chuckled. 'No one to see what you're up to.'

'Granny! It's not like that.'

'No?'

Oran sighed. There was no point in trying to hide things from her grandmother. She could see to the heart of you.

'I'm going to visit my teacher,' she said.

'Your teacher?'

Oran shifted uncomfortably from one foot to the other. 'She's a citharist. Like me and you.'

Her grandmother's brow knotted. 'A citharist? Living on Tusk? I thought it was just birds out there.'

'It is. Just birds, and her.'

'And she's teaching you, is she?'

Oran didn't reply.

'Ah,' said Granny, and her cheeks hung heavily. 'Well. Someone has to, don't they?'

'You know I'd rather learn from you,' said Oran quickly. 'If I could.'

'I know.' Her grandmother sat very still for a few moments, her face like cracked and fissured granite. Her fingers twitched absent-mindedly. 'I'll remember how to sing and play, one of these days. You mark my words! Then we'll raise the roof of the Broken Bottle.' She smiled, but the smile didn't reach her eyes. Oran didn't know what to say. There was an uncomfortable pause.

'She's a good player, is she?' Granny added.

'Oh yes,' said Oran.

'Better than you, even?'

'I think so.' She blushed slightly.

'Well, then. Maybe she can teach you something to sing for the Duchess.'

'Yes!' cried Oran, forgetting she was meant to be quiet. 'Yes,' she said again. 'That's why I'm going. You agree with me, don't you? There's a song for everyone.'

Granny half spoke, half sang, as if she only remembered a handful of notes.

Song for sorrow, song for joy,
Songs to build and to destroy;
Song for winter, song for spring,
Songs for all the tides might bring.

So that was how it went, Oran thought. There was a grunt from her parents' bedroom. She looked anxiously over her shoulder. 'I'd better be on my way,' she said. 'Thank you, Granny. I'm glad someone trusts me.'

'Careful how you go, my love,' said her grandmother, reaching for her knitting needles. Then she stopped and said: 'What's her name, your teacher?'

'Bard.'

'Bard?'

Oran nodded. Granny looked like she was about to

say something else but fell into quiet concentration and began casting on with her knitting needles. Oran waited for a moment and rubbed the lump that had already risen on her forehead. It seemed her grandmother was done talking.

'Bye, then,' she said. Granny raised a hand in vague farewell. Oran ducked through the front door, closed it quietly behind her, and set off for her boat.

When Oran reached the harbour it was eerily quiet. The Duchess's ship hadn't left yet, but there was no one on deck and no one on the quayside. All the fishing boats were still tied up, looking empty and abandoned. It seemed the islanders had taken the mayoress's advice to heart. *When tomorrow comes, you lock your doors.* A lone gull wheeled around the lighthouse and cried out once, twice, as if to ask where everybody had gone.

She looked at the Duchess's frigate. She clenched her fists and sang to herself.

Song for waking, song for sleep,
Song to make the Duchess weep.

There was a moment when she considered storming aboard the ship there and then, confronting the Duchess while she was still in her nightgown. But from somewhere she heard an echo of Alick's worrisome voice and decided that, yes, that probably would make things worse. And besides, she really didn't know what she would sing. That was a new and unpleasant feeling.

Oran went looking for where she'd tied up her boat the previous night. It looked a wreck compared to the neat, coloured fishing boats, but she didn't care. It had originally been built for her by her da, but as she'd got bolder and sailed further, she'd made many improvements of her own. These mostly took the form of thick, heavy planks of wood, nailed haphazardly over the holes that had started appearing in the hull. Recently Oran had started adding extra timber even where there *weren't* any holes, as a preventative measure, and as result the boat was as tough as a man-o'-war. It was almost as wide as it was long, and it prickled with nails and staples she hadn't hammered in properly, prompting her da to rename it the *Urchin*. He joked that if she ever encountered a whale out in the open sea, the whale would come off worse.

The knot in the rope was a mess. She fiddled for a moment, cursed, sucked her fingers, then took her da's knife from her belt and sliced it clean through. She paddled out of the harbour and raised the mast. The sail was still waterlogged from the storm, but once it was unfurled it caught the wind with a loud snap, and the *Urchin* leapt hungrily into the blue

The sea was in a far better mood than the previous night. What few waves there were seemed to part gently before the boat's keel, to offer up a route over the deep. The sun and the salt and the cold air almost made Oran forget the trouble at home. The Duchess, the ghasts, her maw's worries – it all seemed insignificant in the vastness of the ocean.

With a southerly wind, it was an hour to Tusk. For the majority of the journey the sea was truly fathomless, a blue so deep it looked like squid ink. It stayed fair and bright all the way. This was not entirely a good thing. In a squall, you could see the dangers – all you had to worry about was the waves and the weather. On a day like today, when the sea was like a millpond, the sunlight illuminated strange shapes and colours below the surface: old creatures from an older world, that neither understood nor cared for her. She fixed her eyes on the horizon and kept up a one-sided conversation with her cithara.

Tusk rose from the water like a broken bone. Its sides were pale and sheer, with the exception of the Bad Steps, a series of spiralling ledges that offered the only route to the top of the island. Most of them were green with grass and moss, or bright blue with the plumage of nesting galleon birds. As Oran approached, two of them flew out to investigate, a pair of swooping eclipses. Their wingspan was bigger than the boat, their bills deep enough to swallow Oran whole.

'Ahoy there!' called Oran. 'Don't worry about me. Here to see Bard.'

They made low clucking noises and returned to their nests, apparently satisfied.

The reefs at the base of Tusk were treacherous, and Oran took care to lower the mast and paddle herself through the maze of rocks and currents. As the island took her into its cold shadow, she heard the hollow tones of Bard's sea organ, a set of pipes cut into the cliffs that sounded when struck by the waves. The instrument played a low, jaunty fanfare for her arrival.

She tied the boat to a needle of rock, shouldered her cithara, and jumped out into the shallows. From there she sidled around the rock pools until she reached the cave that Bard had made her home.

She called out, 'Bard?'

The only reply was the echo of Oran's voice. She went deeper into the cave. There were blubber lamps in most of the alcoves, but after so long on the bright sea it still took her eyes some time to adjust to the darkness.

'Bard?'

A high-pitched whistle arose from nowhere and cut through the low drone of the sea organ. Bard had left her kettle boiling. Oran crossed the slick rocks to where Bard had spread out her blankets and lifted the kettle out of the flames. She waited. The place was deserted.

Oran left the cave and went around the edge of the island until she found the bottom of the Bad Steps. She began to climb.

Each step was somewhere between five and ten feet high, and most were much taller than her. Even the firmer ones seemed to shift beneath her feet, as though the island was trying to shrug her off. One side of the rock was always out of the sun, and here the ledges were slick and damp. On the other side, there were the piles of bird droppings to navigate. And all the time the wind was snatching at your clothes, your skein, your hair, trying to throw you back into the sea.

She came across Bard unexpectedly, a little below the top of the island. She was sitting in the nest of a galleon bird, silhouetted against the sky, a hundred feet above the sea.

'Bard!' said Oran. 'It's me.'

'I saw you come in, my dear,' said Bard. 'You certainly know how to handle that boat of yours. Masterfully done.'

Oran glowed with pride.

'Come,' said Bard. 'Sit here.'

Oran climbed up the next step, then awkwardly shuffled into place next to Bard. She swung her legs out over the waves crashing far below. When she looked beside her, she saw Bard was cradling an egg the size of her head.

'It's gone cold,' said Bard. She looked down at the egg, and then up at Oran.

It was impossible to tell how old Bard was from her face. It was as knotted and split as driftwood, and her skin had a faint green-blue tint that in some lights made her look radiant, and in others made her look ill. Her long grey hair had a thick crust of salt, and barely moved with the wind.

She was obviously waiting for Oran to say something.

'Is there something wrong with it?'

Bard stroked the surface of the egg. She had fingers like Oran's. The rest of her was tall and slender too, wrapped in a sealskin robe from neck to toe.

'It was abandoned,' she said. 'The father flew away to find food, but never came back. The mother waited as long as she could, until she was weak with hunger. And then she also left. She had no choice. The egg was exposed to the storm last night. The wind and rain were too cold. And now it too is cold.'

She handed it to Oran. It was incredibly heavy.

'Poor old egg,' she said quietly.

'Tell me, Oran,' said Bard, 'do you think you could sing the song of this?'

'What? Me? Now?'

'Do you think,' she said, 'you could sing a song that contained all the sorrow of this little creature that never was?'

'I . . .' She stared at the egg. 'I don't know.'

'Listen.'

Oran listened. She put her ear to the shell. It was smooth and slightly ridged, like a mussel. She couldn't hear anything.

Then Bard began to sing. It began as a low humming, and then split into two notes, then three, then four. Her voice contained all the harmonies of a stringed instrument, and the crags echoed the sound back again until the one woman sounded like a vast choir. The lower registers thrummed like the bass notes of the sea organ; the higher voices sounded like ghast-song.

It was the most beautiful, melancholy music Oran had ever heard. Her heart ached. Her eyes began to fill with tears.

'Stop . . .' she tried to say, but when she made the shape of the word no sound came out.

Bard did not stop. She could have been singing for a few moments; she could have been singing for days. Oran lost all sense of time. All she was aware of was a slight warmth on her back, as her cithara resonated in its case.

'*Stop . . .*'

The timbre of the music changed, almost without her noticing. It was like the arrival of the dawn. There was warmth between her hands now.

Oran sobbed, and laughed, and sobbed again, as the shell cracked and a tiny inquisitive eye peered out. She helped to peel back the fragments, which were thick and hard as fired clay. The chick tapped from the other side, and out came a sticky, shining beak, the shape of a shoe. She lifted the top of the egg. The bird clucked and blinked at her, and she laughed again.

Bard drew her song quietly to a close and sat looking at her lap. Oran said nothing. There was nothing to say. She cleaned the chick up as best she could and laid it in the nest between them. They listened to the waves and the calls of the other galleon birds.

Bard turned to her and finally spoke. 'Right,' she said. 'Cup of tea?'

≥6≤

Bard poured from the kettle into two tortoiseshell cups and handed one to Oran.

'I wasn't expecting you,' she said. 'We only saw each other yesterday.'

'I wasn't expecting to come.'

'Are you here for a lesson?'

'No. Maybe. I don't know. Something's happened at home. I need your help.'

'I see.'

Bard settled down on a pile of seal skins. She'd brought the chick down from its nest and it sat beside her on the blankets. Its huge shoebill was gaping silently.

'Does your mother know you're here?' she asked.

Oran put her nose to her cup of tea, took a sip, and winced at the saltiness of it. 'No,' she said, licking her lips.

'She'll be worried.'

'I know.'

Bard plucked a tiny fish out of the rock pool beside her, ate it, chewed it, then let it fall into the chick's open mouth. The chick gurgled appreciatively. There was a moment or two of silence while Oran stared at the surface of her tea.

'You're here about the Duchess, aren't you?' Bard said.

Oran looked up. 'You know?'

'I heard.'

'Heard what?'

'The silence. She brought it with her from the Headland.'

'Ach,' said Oran. 'I wish I had your ears.'

Bard laughed. 'Tell me: what does Her Grace want with the musicians of Little Drum?'

'She wants us to stop singing.'

Bard frowned. 'Stop singing what, exactly?'

'Everything! She's threatening to take our instruments. She said she'd evict us if we didn't do what she said.'

'I see.'

'She can't do that, though, can she? Little Drum is our home. It belongs to us.'

'I'm afraid that's not strictly true,' said Bard. 'All of the Far Isles – even this one – belong to the Duchess. You are only caretakers of Little Drum, going back hundreds and hundreds of years. In the beginning you were supposed to give a portion of what you farmed or fished to the Headland, in return for your right to live on the island. No one has insisted on tithes for a very long time now. Most people have simply forgotten the agreement ever existed. It seems the Duchess has, conveniently, just remembered the details.'

'So they can evict us?'

'Worse. If they evict you, there's nowhere in the islands you can resettle, because the same laws will apply everywhere. You'll be cast out completely. You'll have to go as far south as the Green Sea before you find a land where no one has heard of the Duchess.'

'How do you know all this?'

'I'm a good listener.'

Oran looked glumly into the water and took another mouthful of tea. This one had a piece of seaweed in it. In fact, she began to suspect that seaweed was the only ingredient in what Bard called 'tea'.

'Another cup?' Bard asked.

'Um. No. Thank you. Very nice.'

'Mind if I have one?'

She shook her head. The woman went and busied herself in the hollows of the cave, throwing various things into the kettle that Oran couldn't see. Then she came back and slung it over the fire between them. Oran waited for her to say something else, but all she did was poke at the contents of the kettle and occasionally stroke the chick's head with a finger.

'I thought you could help us,' Oran said at last.

Bard looked at her over the kettle. Beneath her ridged brow her eyes had gone a strange colour – or rather, they had no colour at all. They were as clear as the shallows around a reef and reflected the light in strange, undulating ways. She pulled her sealskin robe tighter around her chin and lowered her voice.

'How's that?' she said.

'Well. You know how you said that there's a song for everything.'

'Everything *has* a song. Its own music. That's not quite the same thing.'

Oran didn't see the difference. 'Right. Well. I was thinking, in that case, there must be a song to change the Duchess's mind.'

Bard gave a laugh like a seal's bark. Oran collapsed a little inside.

'Why's that so funny?'

'I'm sorry, my dear. I shouldn't laugh. But the Duchess will not be swayed by any kind of song. She hates music. Every last instrument, every last note.'

'But *why*?'

'She is afraid of it.'

'Nonsense! No one's afraid of music.'

'She's tone-deaf, Oran. There's no such thing on your island, because music is in your bones. But things are different on the Headland. Samhair cannot sing, cannot play, cannot dance. Why, she cannot even listen. Music is something that is forever beyond her understanding. She fears it, because she doesn't understand it.'

'You say that like you know her . . .'

'I do,' Bard said, taking another gulp of tea. 'At least, I did. Why do you think I'm on this island, Oran? She was the person who put me here.'

'The *Duchess* did?'

'Been a full year, now. I was the finest musician on the Headland, so naturally I was the first to go. Exiled, on pain of death.' Bard's eyes had changed again. Churned sand in stormy waters. 'Worse than that,' she added, as not much more than an afterthought. 'She took the whalebone cithara from me.'

Oran gasped. 'The whalebone cithara? Not *the* whalebone cithara?'

Bard raised her salt-crusted brows. 'You've heard of it?'

'*Heard* of it? It's one of my favourite stories!'

'And how does that story go, according to the people of Little Drum?'

Oran knew it by heart. She'd learnt it at her maw's knee, before she'd even been old enough to hold her cithara upright.

'It's one of the First Instruments. One of the nine the Chorus made for the world, after they'd sung the sea and the land into being. There were nine musicians, kings and queens, who were meant to rule over the lands and the seas. They got an instrument each. But they didn't listen to each other, and they wouldn't play in harmony, and everything went wrong.' She paused, because Bard was listening to her with such concentration. 'So the Chorus took them back and hid them on Little Drum. Under the earth. That's why we're all such good musicians. That's why we have the ghasts. Because the instruments are still playing, deep underground.' Bard didn't move. 'That's the gist, anyway.'

'And?' said her teacher. 'What next?'

'That's the end. They've stayed in the Great Barrow because no one's allowed to play them.'

'Well, it can't be right, can it?'

'What do you mean?'

'If no one's allowed to play them, how did I end up with the whalebone cithara?'

'Oh. Yes.' She frowned. 'How *did* you end up with it?'

Bard thought for a moment. 'I suppose you could say it found me, Oran. It was always said that the First Instruments would find new owners when the right players came along. We heard each other across the sea, the whalebone cithara and I. It sought me out.'

Oran didn't understand what she meant by that, but still shook her head in wonder. Her maw was always telling her she was too gullible. But as she got older she was starting to realize that more stories were true than were not.

'And it was the real thing?'

'Real enough to give me these calluses,' said Bard. She held out her hand. Her fingertips were rough and hard as pumice.

'What does it sound like?'

The old woman looked far away. Her eyes were calm now. They had as many moods as the sea. When she spoke they became like opals, a deep and otherworldly blue, flecked with a thousand other colours. 'It has a tone unlike any other instrument in the world. It plays a music so pure it touches even the hardest hearts and minds. And I don't just mean people, Oran. The sea, the winds, the trees, the rocks. When the whalebone cithara plays, the whole world listens. It plays the Old Music, you see.'

'The Old Music?'

Bard nodded. '*True* music. The music that is the essence of all things.'

'Was that what you were singing before? About the bird, and the egg?'

Bard looked at the chick. Its eyes were closed in an expression that looked like bliss. 'It wasn't a song *about* the bird. It was the song *of* the bird. Do you see the difference? That is what the Old Music is. The music that makes up the world.' She paused. 'That's what I've been teaching you. Or rather, what the whalebone cithara has been teaching you, through me. Everything I know, I learnt from that instrument.'

Oran liked that idea. That she was not simply learning ballads and lays, but the substance beneath them: the melodies and harmonies at the heart of the world. What a thought – that, with a flourish of her fingers, she might call the sea itself to listen to her!

'Do you think the Duchess would listen to the whalebone cithara?'

Bard studied her very closely. It made Oran a little uncomfortable, to sit cross-legged under the weight of that gaze. It was as if the woman was listening to every beat of her heart. At last, she smiled. 'She would have no choice,' she said.

'Then I should go and find it!' said Oran, leaping to

her feet. 'Even if she doesn't listen to it, everyone else would. I could play a song to raise a mutiny against her. And failing that, I could conjure a wave to wash her back where she came from!'

'You could, could you, Oran?'

Oran's mouth hung open for a moment. Her cithara was making a noise like nails on a blackboard. 'I mean *you*, obviously. Not me. You could play it. It's your instrument.'

Bard stared at her, still as a stone, and for a moment Oran felt as if she was looking at some kind of sea creature, ancient, unfathomably alien.

'I'm sure I could think of some song or other,' she said.

'Where is the cithara now?' asked Oran.

'Unless I'm mistaken, it's still in the Duchess's palace. Her men stole it from me while I slept. Otherwise I would have played it for her when she tried to exile me.'

'But she didn't destroy it?'

'No. She keeps confiscated instruments locked in a tower. A kind of museum. Trophies of the hunt.' She paused. 'Funny really. Must be the most exquisite collection of instruments in all the Four Seas, and she can't play a note on any of them.'

Oran spoke without thinking – something else her maw wished she'd grow out of. 'I'll get it for you!' she said. 'I can take the *Urchin*.'

Bard laughed again. 'I don't think you realize how far it is to the Headland, my dear.'

'She'll hold up. I've made some improvements to her.'

'That is very kind of you, Oran, and very brave, but the journey is a dangerous one.' She sat still for a while longer, examining her long fingers, bending them one at a time. The sea organ droned at the mouth of the cave. 'Though,' she added, 'I can think of no other way to convince the Duchess of her folly.'

'Then I don't have a *choice*, do I?'

'Perhaps not.'

'I'll do it. I'll find the whalebone cithara.'

Bard chuckled. 'I'd wager of all the islanders, you'd be the most likely to succeed.'

'I'll start packing as soon as I get home!'

'One thing, though,' said Bard. 'It would be best not to tell anyone else that you're going. If the location of the whalebone cithara becomes common knowledge, the world and his wife will come looking for it too.'

'Right-o.'

'And your maw,' she added. 'Best not tell your maw. We don't want to make her any more worried than she already is.'

Oran put her thumb and forefinger together and

mimed sealing her lips.

Bard's face shone. 'You are a wonder, my dear,' she said, and her words warmed Oran like the sun rising. 'Come, I am full of hope for the first time since I came to this dismal place. Let us sing in defiance of the Duchess! I was listening hard to the lobsters, last night. They taught me a new song, an interesting little dance. Difficult without ten legs, but we can try. May I?' Bard held out her hand.

It was frowned upon to let anyone else play your birth instrument, but Bard was different. Oran loved to hear her play, and the only instrument Bard had was a very crude thing she'd sculpted from driftwood and old fishing line. She undid the clasps on her case and handed the cithara to her teacher.

Bard began to play, explaining the strange finger-ings and bizarre intervals that on Little Drum might not even have been thought of as music at all. Oran felt doors and windows opening into dark and unused rooms in her mind. Like she was seeing and hearing the world properly for the first time.

She lost all sense of time as they played and sang. At some point, though, she became aware that she was thinking of her mother. She pictured her frayed with anxiety, pacing the harbour and looking for her daughter on the horizon.

'I should probably go,' she said, stopping her song

abruptly. The sun had set, and the sky outside was the colour of heather.

'Hmmm.' Bard went to the mouth of the cave. 'No. It's too late. The waters between here and Little Drum are treacherous after dark, and the things that live in them more treacherous still.'

Oran looked out over the slow, dark heave of the sea. Part of her wanted to be home, next to the fire; part of her was more excited than ever to be on her own and doing what she loved most.

'Can I stay here, then?' she asked.

'Of course, my dear. I'm not going to ask you to bed down in the bottom of your boat. Though, to look at it, I'm sure it's one of the safest places in the Far Isles.'

So, for the first time, Oran stayed the night on Tusk. She and Bard spoke and sang of many things, but always came back to the story of the whalebone cithara and the Old Music. Bard told her of the things it could do, described what it looked like, even drew her two simple maps, one of the Court and one of the Headland, on a piece of dried sea lettuce.

When Oran finally curled up under her sealskin blanket, the cave was brighter than it had been all day. The inlet was full of luminous fish and corals and anemones, shining blue, green and violet. A small glowing squid rose to the surface and observed her where she lay – puzzled, no doubt, as to how such creatures could live in complete darkness. Oran wriggled under the covers and it darted away.

Such strange things there were in the world, she thought. She wondered how many more she would see when she sailed to the Headland.

7

O ran woke up when the day was still a vague, grey thought at the edge of the ocean. She'd slept fitfully. The previous night had seemed like a fever dream, weirdly lit by the cave's nocturnal inhabitants.

It was dark now, and cold. There was one thought that loomed larger than the Duchess, the Headland or the whalebone cithara – and that was breakfast. Oran was ravenous. Bard had made them 'supper' the previous evening, but all three of them – Oran, Bard and the newborn chick – had dined on the same fishy pulp.

She crept through the gloom towards Bard's seal furs and whispered, 'Bard, I'm going to go home now.'

There was no answer.

'Bard?'

Oran nudged the furs with her toe, but Bard wasn't among them. She went to the edge of the cave, thinking she might have to climb the Bad Steps yet again, but she found the old woman standing waist-deep in the sea, one hand on Oran's boat.

'I can hear it,' she said, without turning around.

'Hear what?'

'My cithara. It's calling out. It knows you're coming.'

Oran shivered. Sailing to the Headland suddenly seemed a less appealing prospect in the grey light of the early morning, when the sea was chill and leaden.

'Why don't you come with me?' she said suddenly. 'There's room for two in here.'

'No, no,' said Bard. 'I'd be thrown in prison the moment I stepped on to the Headland. I am not welcome there. My presence would endanger the whole expedition.'

'Oh yes,' Oran said. 'I hadn't thought of that.' Perhaps she could bring Alick with her? It was possible, in theory. There was no one else she could think of.

'It is a marvellous thing you're doing,' said Bard.

'We'll show the Duchess just how afraid she should be of music!'

Oran put her cithara and the maps that Bard had drawn into the boat, and tucked them under her seat. She picked up the paddle and prepared to lever herself away from the rocks.

Bard suddenly grabbed her wrist. 'One last thing.'

Oran looked up. Bard's fingers were impossibly strong. 'What's that?'

'Don't try to play it yourself. If you find it, bring it straight here. It is an instrument of great power, and dangerous in the hands of the wrong player.'

Oran tried and failed to hide her disappointment. 'All right,' she said.

'Promise me. The whalebone cithara found *me*. I am Bard. It cannot be played by another.'

'I promise,' said Oran, and saying the words felt like heaving two rocks into the boat with her.

'Good.' Bard let go of her arm and smiled. 'Be careful, dear girl. And be quick. Things move apace on Little Drum. I would sing you a favourable wind, but I'm afraid the song would not come out right without my instrument . . .'

Oran's heart leapt at the idea of being able to sing the wind itself; then sank again when she remembered the promise she'd just made.

*

The *Urchin* laboured out into the open water, and Oran put up the mast and let down the sail. The sea was sluggish and every wave was heavy as old snow. Once she was free of the reefs around Tusk she turned back to wave Bard goodbye, but the woman was gone. The island receded, and Oran continued to check over her shoulder, hoping to see her teacher climbing the Bad Steps, nimble as a mountain torc, but there was no sign of her.

When she arrived back at Little Drum the Duchess's frigate had gone, but in its place were two more big-bellied ships from the Headland. The seafront was crawling with men in scarlet shawls and pantaloons. The Duchess's family skein was a horrid thing, Oran thought, its pattern violent and jagged. It was the complete opposite of her own skein, bright green threads curling and flowing through a blue background. Her grandmother had taught her to weave it herself, since she couldn't teach her to play. Both weaving and playing were strangely similar, Oran thought, rhythmic and calming, existing somewhere between thinking and dreaming. And they both required quick fingers.

The Headlanders didn't see her as she tied up the *Urchin*. She looked to where the pier met the quayside. Two of them were pushing a cart along the seafront. It was full of instruments.

She quickly hid in one of the boathouses, her pulse hot and throbbing. She had to hide her cithara, which was already trembling on her back. She *hushed* it, then found an old lobster pot that was just large enough to accommodate the instrument and its case, and so encrusted with barnacles no one would see what was inside. She took the lobster pot under one arm and came back out on to the quay. Two more Headlanders rattled past with another trolley of instruments. Their many-coloured lacquers and enamels caught the sun like heaps of jewellery. They knocked discordantly against each other. It was unbearable to hear.

Oran looked at her feet and began the climb back home. When she got to her front door, she found Alick outside, peering through the cottage's window. There were raised voices inside.

She set down the lobster pot. 'Alick,' she hissed.

He whirled around, his outline fuzzed with his surprise. 'Oran!'

'You should remember this, next time you decide to sneak up on me.'

He stared at her for a moment, mouth open. 'Where've you *been*?'

'I told you, I went to see Bard.'

'You've been gone all night!'

'I lost track of time.'

'Everyone is out of their minds! Don't you think

we've got enough to worry about already?'

'Well, I'm here now.'

Alick looked at the lobster pot. 'What's that for?'

'I hid my cithara in it. I've just come from the harbour and—'

'They've taken everyone's instruments. I know. And you weren't here.'

Oran felt a flush of guilt, but said quickly: 'I can put it right. I know I can. What did the ghasts say?'

Alick sighed and his brows did an extraordinary dance of confusion and worry. 'The ancestors agreed that someone should make the island's case to the Duchess. They decided that a delegation should be sent to the Court. And they decided that you should go with them.'

Oran yelped. She couldn't believe it. She'd spent half the night wondering how she would make a journey so perilous, plotting her route between the islands, calculating tide times, drafting the letter she'd leave for her mother, but now she needn't worry about any of those things. And better yet, she had the ghasts' blessing to go!

'Alick! This is *exactly* what I need!'

She again tried to throw her arms around Alick, and again found herself embracing thin air. It took a moment for his features to appear again, and when they did it was clear he didn't share Oran's delight.

'What?' she said. 'What's wrong?'

'I don't think you'll be setting sail any time soon,' he said miserably. 'Your maw—'

'What about my maw?'

'She—'

Alick didn't finish. There was another volley of shouting from inside the cottage. He shrank back, like an octopus into its den.

'I'm going in there,' said Oran, opening the lobster pot and retrieving her cithara case.

'I don't think that is a good idea,' said Alick.

She flung the door open anyway. Inside were her parents, her grandmother and the two mayors.

'What are you all yelling about?' said Oran.

Everyone turned to look at her, apart from her mother. That was a bad sign. The mayors gave awkward 'hello's. Her granny was gutting fish in the corner. The room seemed emptier than it should have, as if there was a family member missing. Oran kept looking around, thinking she'd see a set of bagpipes bundled into a corner, her maw's fiddle tucked behind an armchair. But there were no instruments in the house, save the one she was carrying. She hugged it to her chest, and it quivered in its heart-shaped case.

'The answer is *no*,' her maw said into the silence.

'But, Cora,' said the mayor, 'it's what the ghasts have

decided. You're not just going to ignore them, are you? We're bound by the Moot.'

'If I need to know when to sow my crops, or when to pasture the torcs, or when a storm is going to break, I'll talk to the ghasts. If I'm missing a final verse for my harvest song, then I'll talk to the ghasts. When it comes to looking after my daughter, I'll make my own decisions, thank you.'

Oran was stunned. The number of times her maw had lectured her on respecting her ancestors!

'But she's the best musician on the island,' said the mayoress. 'And the only one with an instrument now. It just makes sense.'

'She's not going.' Her maw folded her arms. 'She's just a girl, and a wayward one, at that.'

'Then what do we do?' said the mayor. 'We can't just leave things as they are. No instruments, no songs. I don't know how long it'll be till the ghasts start to leave us.' His voice suddenly rattled like a cracked pot. 'Not even the ghasts know.'

'We can send a delegation. They'll just have to talk, like the Headlanders do.'

The mayors looked at each other and frowned.

'Cora,' said the mayoress, 'there's no dispute on this island that has *ever* been solved without a song. I tried to talk to her in the Broken Bottle, and you saw how far that got me.'

'My mind's made up,' said Oran's maw.

The cottage went very quiet again. There was the plop of fish guts into Granny's bucket. Her face wore a look of intense concentration, though it didn't seem to be the fish-gutting that concerned her.

'I'd like to go,' said Oran.

'You're not leaving this house, young lady.'

'Why not?'

Her mother finally faced her, and all of a sudden it was like they were the only two in the room.

'Even if I weren't angrier with you than I've ever been' – the mayors fiddled nervously with their fish-bone necklaces – 'and even if I weren't in pieces over my instrument, and your father's instrument, and everybody else's wretched instrument, I *still* wouldn't let you go. The journey is far too dangerous. Storms, currents. The Greymers.'

Oran wanted to protest, but her mother sounded so grief-stricken it was hard to muster anything particularly forceful.

'You're always telling me the Greymers aren't real . . .' she said.

'The plan is ridiculous, anyway,' her maw continued. 'The Duchess won't listen to any song. She hates singing. That's the whole point.'

'I could *make* her listen,' said Oran.

'You're not as good a player as you think you are.'

'But, Maw!' Oran fought hard to keep the frustration out of her voice, knowing it would only make her sound more childish. She couldn't mention the whalebone cithara either. Couldn't mention Bard. There was little she could say in her favour. 'You're *always* telling me to respect my elders, and now your elders are telling you I should go to the Headland and you're ignoring them!' She paused, then muttered: 'It's a load of rotgut!'

'That's *enough*, Oran.' It was the first thing her father had said since she'd arrived.

'Don't take her side, Da!'

The mayors exchanged tired looks. The husband's fingers twitched absent-mindedly on his missing instrument. It was so sad to see. How could her maw be so stubborn, when everything looked and sounded so bleak?

'You obviously have a lot to talk about,' said the mayoress. 'We will give your answer to the ghasts, Cora. I expect they won't be very pleased. Of course, if you change your mind . . .'

A pair of narrowed eyes was all it took. The mayors bowed quickly and scurried out of the door

'I don't know what to do with you, girl,' Oran's maw said. 'You're breaking my old heart.'

Before Oran could reply she shook her head and went out into the kitchen, where she began violently clanging pans and slamming cupboards.

'She loves you, Oran,' said her da. 'That's all.'

'I wish she'd trust me as much as she loves me,' said Oran.

'I think she'd trust you more if you didn't keep running away all the time.'

'But that's *why* I keep running away! To prove that she can trust me!'

Her father smiled sadly and shook his head.

'I mean it, Da,' said Oran. 'How am I supposed to show that I can make my own decisions if she won't ever *let* me make my own decisions?'

'You were gone for a day and a night. Didn't leave a note. Didn't tell anyone where you were going.' Oran looked over at Granny, but Granny's mind was elsewhere. 'I would say that wasn't one of your better decisions. We were all thinking the worst.'

'I just wanted to help.'

'Help how? Where have you even been?'

Oran looked at her fingernails with great concentration. She felt her father's warm, rough hand on her cheek.

'Oran. Don't hide things from us. Not now. Please.'

She didn't know what to say. She'd sworn to Bard that she would keep her existence a secret. And she'd sworn that she wouldn't tell anyone about the whalebone cithara. But her da looked so sad.

Everyone looked so sad.

She was saved from having to answer by a sharp knock at the door. Oran and her father jumped. Granny looked up from her bucket of fish heads. Her maw came back from the kitchen. All of them afraid to move or speak in the fragile silence.

Another knock, as if someone was pelting the cottage with stones. Oran stared at the glass porthole set into the top half of the door. All she saw was sky, and the waving branches of trees. Whoever had called on them was no taller than a child.

8

'Open up in there!' said Magmalley. His voice had a buzzing quality, like a trapped insect.

Oran clutched her cithara to her chest, paralysed with terror.

Her da replied in his booming bass: 'You've already been to this house. Let us mourn our instruments in peace.' He mouthed to Oran: *hide*. It took her a moment or two to remember how to move her legs.

'Your daughter has recently returned,' said Magmalley. 'She was seen at the harbour.'

'Well, she isn't here!' said her da.

'The mayors informed me they spoke to her moments ago in this very house. So how is that? Are they drunk?'

Oran saw, through the little round window, the faces of his guards. One of them cupped a hand and put his face to the glass. She felt a throb of panic. She ducked out of sight and ran through the kitchen to the back door.

Outside the torcs were lazing around in their paddock, rooting up chestnuts and other buried treasure with their enormous snouts. Oran always found something reassuring about their simple, untroubled lives. She crept into the herd and hid among their warm, woolly bodies. She waited. The animals' flanks rose and fell like bellows.

'Alick?' she whispered.

'I'm not coming in there,' he said, from somewhere outside the herd. He was always convinced they were moments from stampede.

'Then keep a lookout!'

Over the roaring of the torcs' breath she could just hear her parents' voices. They sounded like their instruments – her father's slow and droning, her mother's quick and taut. They also sounded exhausted.

Alick drifted among the animals. One of them scratched itself and he gave it a wide berth, watching apprehensively.

'He's searching the house,' he said to Oran.

'Oh squid . . .'

'I think you need to find a better hiding place than this. While he's occupied.'

'Where can I go, though? The Headlanders are everywhere on the island. You said so yourself.'

'What about the Great Barrow? He's not allowed in there.'

'*I'm* not allowed in there.'

'Maybe I could give you permission. I know I'm young, but I *am* a ghast.'

Oran thought about this. The Great Barrow was the one place in the whole of Little Drum she hadn't explored. It was forbidden to enter it, except to perform the funeral rites.

Magmalley's buzzing wasp-voice came from the kitchen: 'I know you are here. You're only getting your parents into more trouble.'

Oran didn't move.

Magmalley went on, 'They are *technically* harbouring a criminal.'

Even if she went to the Great Barrow with her cithara, what then? She couldn't hide there for ever.

'Of course, the Duchess might even grant them a reprieve for giving you up. You were, after all, the one who instigated that obnoxious song the other night.'

Oran's heart and stomach lurched at the same time. She stood up. The torcs got up with her, disturbed, and went blundering over the paddock in all directions. Magmalley was there, on the doorstep of the kitchen, looking straight at her.

'Ah! Good morning!' he said, squinting against the sunlight.

It was nearly midday now, and hot, but he was still in all his finery: knee socks, garters, woollen pantaloons, woollen jerkin, skein and feather bonnet. Sweat coursed down the sides of his nose, which he mopped obsessively with a handkerchief. At his back were half a dozen Headlanders in their red livery, and behind them she saw the worried faces of her parents.

'What a jewel of a day! And they told me the Far Isles were all mist and gloom.'

'What do you want?' Oran said, though she knew exactly what he wanted.

'I was sorry to miss you yesterday. After your performance in the tavern I was very much hoping to talk to you in person. But when we arrived you'd gone and run away. Your poor mother. She was so distraught!'

'I didn't run away,' she said. She balled her fists until it hurt.

'Evidently not,' said Magmalley. 'Here you are, safe and sound! What a relief.' He gave a predatory smile.

'Now, if you don't mind, yours is the only instrument that is outstanding on our inventory.'

Oran took a small pace backwards. 'You don't need to do this,' she said.

'I'm afraid we do.' He cocked his head. 'I know it must be difficult for you to understand, being so young.'

'I understand well enough.'

'Do you?' he said, looking amused.

'Your Duchess is afraid,' she said, thinking of what Bard had said. 'She's afraid of music because she doesn't understand it. And she's jealous too. She's jealous that we have something she can't have.'

Alick glimmered beside her. 'I don't think this is a good idea,' he said.

The amusement on Magmalley's face had faded. 'If she is afraid,' he said, 'she is afraid with good reason. Did you hear the things that came from your mouth? Do you have any idea how dangerous it is spreading lies like that? Songs are not like normal lies – they spread more easily, and they cling more perniciously. They are infectious.'

Oran's cithara seemed to groan on her back.

'And that's just the words,' Magmalley went on. 'Have you ever really *watched* someone listening to music? They seem hardly aware of the world around them. Wild. Drunken. It is hardly a civilized society when everyone is out of their own heads for half of the time. The Duchess's subjects were a disorderly mob when she inherited the Headland. Now its citizens are quiet. They are focused. They are *useful*.'

He folded his arms, satisfied his case had been made. Oran looked at the guards, sweltering in their woollens, then back at Magmalley.

'So you've never enjoyed a song in your life?' she asked him.

His mouth became a very small, a pinprick in his circular face. 'Not that I can remember, no,' he said.

He was lying, Oran knew.

'You don't hum? Or whistle?'

'Absolutely not.'

'What about your men?'

He jerked his head to either side, as if warning them not to reply.

'Were there no shanties on the trip over here?' said Oran. 'It must be three or four days' sailing from the Headland to here. I don't imagine that's much fun. Storms and high winds. You must miss your families.'

'Enough of this,' said Magmalley. 'Your instrument.' He extended his small hand.

'Didn't you allow them a single song to lift their spirits?' She felt her face getting hot. 'Isn't there anything *useful* about that?'

Magmalley tried to take another step forward,

found something brown and wet on the buckle of his shoe, and thought the better of it. He gestured to the other men. 'What are you waiting for? Take it from her!'

They looked up as if woken from a dream, and slowly began to cross the pasture towards Oran.

Alick's outline trembled. 'What now?' he said.

Oran slung her cithara case from her shoulder and undid the clasps. She sat and held it in her lap. She heard her parents protesting from the kitchen, but didn't know if they were shouting at her or at Magmalley.

The instrument was a little out of tune, and Oran's fingers were stiff, but the first notes were still enough to stop the Headlanders in their tracks.

Magmalley looked on, astonished. 'What are you doing?' he said. 'How dare you!'

Oran played without thinking. It was no tune that anyone had heard before. She listened, as Bard had taught her, for that music that lay between her and the men in the field. True music. She listened for the Headlanders' melancholy, their silence, their homesickness, and wove them into melody and harmony. She listened for her parents' sadness, and her own, and all the islanders'. She found herself singing, but what the words were she didn't know.

The Headlanders wavered. They shook their heads

and dabbed their eyes with their skeins. Lord Magmalley shoved a pair of jewelled plugs in his ears.

'Stop that!' he cried.

The more carefully Oran listened, the more easily the music came to her. She heard the men's tears and echoed them delicately, brought order and beauty to their sadness. They hunched over and began to sob all the more.

'I said, *stop*!' Lord Magmalley marched towards Oran. She was aware of him only as a vague presence on the edge of the song. As he came closer the sound of his voice cut through the music like a snapped string.

She felt a tug. She missed a beat, and the tune faltered. Then another, and Lord Magmalley wrenched her birth instrument from her hands. She heard her parents' voices again, wild and tremulous. With the ragged edges of the tune still trailing in the air, Magmalley swung the cithara against the trunk of the tree.

It held together at first. One of its curved arms became crooked, the bridge came loose, the strings slackened. He hurled it again, more violently, and this time the wood snapped completely with a sound like bones breaking. Still he didn't stop. He smashed the instrument against the tree over and over until it was in five or six splintered pieces, a couple of them held loosely together by the strings.

Oran watched dumbly as he walked away. She felt her face, head, chest suddenly overcome with a sickening, white-hot fever. At some point her da came over to her, but he was a shadow, and spoke to her as though through several feet of earth. He tried to pick up one of the pieces. She screamed, and he placed it back in the dirt.

When she finally looked up, perhaps an hour later, the Headlanders were gone and the whole island was silent.

⋙9⋘

Oran had been bereaved once before, when her grandfather's heart had given out. He'd been climbing the sea cliffs in search of gulls' eggs. Back then, she had only found comfort in playing her cithara. What was she to do now, when her cithara was the thing she was grieving for?

The pieces of her birth instrument had been collected together in its case and placed above the hearth. Oran couldn't bring herself to look at them. She stared into the fire instead. They had lit it, but it seemed to give no heat at all.

Outside, the Duchess's men went on their rounds through the town. It was said they'd gone up north too. They'd been stationed in the villages of the cockle-pickers, among the ships of the whalers – men and women who rarely came ashore. Magmalley hadn't given them earplugs, but rather the opposite – they carried small brass ear trumpets, which they used to listen for unsanctioned songs and music. Old Crake, the beet farmer, had been given a black eye for humming to himself while gathering in his crop.

Oran watched a red skein flutter past the cottage window.

'We'll sing tonight, instruments or no,' said her maw.

Nobody answered. Oran looked at her. Her mother seemed half her normal size. All the defiance gone out of her. Her fingers twitched out of habit, missing something vital between them.

Her da came out of the kitchen with a tray of warm torc milk and offered the drinks round. 'At least they left you the pieces,' he said. 'Someone might be able to fix it.'

'Not likely,' said Alick. He'd been mooning around the place since it had happened. On the one hand it was nice to have someone to commiserate with her, but he wasn't helping lift the mood at all.

'I don't know,' said her da. 'I'm sure we can find a

luthier somewhere. If not here, maybe on another island. One of the Five Fingers, maybe.'

'All the best luthiers are on Little Drum,' said Alick.

'Well, there's no harm in asking.'

Oran smiled at her da's optimism, but she had to agree with Alick. There was nothing to be salvaged from so many pieces.

They sat quietly for a little while longer. Oran sipped at her mug of torc milk. Torcs were amazing animals. They were strong and intelligent; their wool was warm and waterproof, and came in a thousand colours; and their milk fortified mind and body like some magic elixir. It was said that on the Headland they ate the torc's meat, but no one ever thought of that in the Far Isles.

She swallowed another mouthful. It lit a fire in her cheeks and her belly.

'So now will you let me go?' she said to her maw.

'Go where, love?'

'To the Headland.'

For a moment it looked like her mother was trying to fan something from the embers of her anger, but in the end she just sighed.

'No, Oran. My mind hasn't changed just because of what's happened. And now – I'm sorry to say – there's even less reason for you to go. You can't sing for the

Duchess without your cithara.'

In fact, thought Oran, the opposite was true. It was more urgent than ever that someone do something about the Duchess. And if she had no birth instrument, the whalebone cithara might make a handsome replacement . . .

She caught herself mid-thought, remembered what Bard had said, and shook the idea from her head.

'Don't shake your head at me, my girl,' said her maw. 'I haven't got the energy for an argument.'

'I wasn't—'

'It's time we started on dinner. Help your da with the tatties.'

Her maw got up and went back to the kitchen. Oran's da followed soon after, leaving Oran with Granny. Alick hovered in the middle of the living room, wringing his hands, not knowing who to side with. If there were two people Oran trusted as much as Bard, it was her grandmother and her best friend. Surely Bard wouldn't begrudge her sharing things with them?

'Granny,' she said, very quietly.

'Yes, my love.'

'You know the First Instruments. The nine that the Chorus gave us.'

Her grandmother suddenly looked very alert. She

blinked a couple of times. 'Of course.'

'They're real, aren't they?'

Again, her grandmother rested for a beat before replying, 'As real as you and me. If they weren't real, we wouldn't be the musicians that we are. And your little friend wouldn't be here at all.'

Alick mouthed a reply, no doubt unhappy at the term 'little friend', but no words came out.

'Why do you ask that, all of a sudden?' said Granny.

'I was wondering if someone could play them now. To help us with the Duchess.'

Her grandmother shook her head, and her long white hair tumbled in front of her face. 'No, Oran. They are sacred things, the instruments. Powerful too. You know the story.'

'Are they really that dangerous?'

Alick was making worried circles around the living room. 'I don't like where you're going with this, Oran,' he said.

'I agree,' said Granny. 'Yes, my love, they *are* that dangerous. They play the Old Music. Do you know why the world is the shape that it is? So much water? So many little pieces of land, scattered about? It's not because the Chorus made it this way. It's because of those first players, who took the Chorus's instruments and sang for their own ends. Sang selfishly. Each their own song, out of tune with the others. Set sea against sea, and land against land. Don't forget, the Chorus used those instruments to make the world – it stands to reason that they might be used to *un*make it, in the wrong hands.'

'But what if they were in the *right* hands?'

'And whose hands are the right hands? Yours?'

Oran didn't answer that.

'There are no right hands,' said her grandmother. Her voice was stronger than Oran had ever heard it. 'And besides, the instruments are deep in the Great Barrow. No one apart from the ghasts has ever laid eyes on them. Isn't that right, Alick?'

'But one of the instruments isn't in the Great Barrow any more,' said Oran. 'The cithara. The whale-bone cithara.'

Granny gave her a piercing look. She seemed twenty years younger, upright and bright-eyed. 'Who told you that?'

'I just heard it.'

'Heard it from whom, Oran?'

'A friend.'

'This "Bard" woman?'

Oran didn't reply.

'Who is she, Oran? How does she know these things?'

Oran had never seen her grandmother so animated. There was something frightening about it. As if

Granny had suddenly cast off some lifelong disguise she'd always worn.

'She said . . . she said she'd played it. She said it was her instrument. It had found her.'

The old woman froze, her lips open a fraction. That made Oran worry even more. She thought, for a few horrible moments, that her grandmother had gone the same way as her grandfather; that Granny's heart had stopped stone-dead in her chest.

At last she took a deep breath in. She never took her eyes off her granddaughter. 'And where,' she asked, 'is the whalebone cithara now?'

'On the Headland. At the Court. I have a map and everything.'

'Then someone needs to bring it back,' said her grandmother.

At this, Oran's maw thundered back into the room. 'No,' she said. '*Stop this.* Right now. I can still hear everything you're saying. I won't let you put any more daft ideas in the girl's head. Oran, I've asked you to peel tatties. Maw, you keep your stories to yourself. We've had enough bad luck as it is without you inviting more upon us. Everybody is staying in this house until the ghasts think of a solution. Have I made myself clear?'

'They've thought of a solution . . .' said Oran.

'A *better* solution,' said her mother. 'One that

doesn't involve my daughter being put at the mercy of the seas.'

She was brandishing a wooden spoon in the hand that would normally have held her fiddle bow. It was a poor replacement. Oran felt sorry for her maw, sorry for herself, sorry for everyone. It only made her more determined. She wouldn't wait any longer. If both Bard and Granny thought it was important to look for the whalebone cithara she didn't need any more persuading. Alick would say it wasn't a good idea, but he never thought anything was a good idea.

'Into the kitchen. Now.'

'Yes, Maw,' Oran said, and took the potato peeler. Her granny watched her go. She obviously had a good deal more to say to her.

Oran and her da stood over the sink in the kitchen. He spoke to her about her broken cithara while handing her potatoes one by one. He was trying to think of luthiers he knew. Oran wasn't listening, though. She was compiling the list of provisions she'd need for a trip to the Headland.

The bells of the town hall rang out midnight. Oran hadn't been to sleep. She slid out of bed, picked up the sack she had filled earlier in the evening – cheese, sausages, dry crackers, apples, two thick sweaters and her grandmother's old waterproof sou'wester – and crept through the darkness of the cottage. The curtains hadn't been drawn and the front room was blue with starlight.

She tiptoed over to the pieces of her cithara and placed her hand on the case. The leather was dead-cold. 'I'm sorry,' she whispered. 'I'll come back soon. And I'll get you fixed.' It felt like a lie. The instrument was silent.

Somebody stirred in her parents' room. Oran left her cithara case where it stood, went to the front door, and took off into the night.

Alick was waiting for her in the street. 'I knew it,' he said. 'I *knew* you were going to do something stupid.'

'Be *quiet*, Alick!' she hissed, drawing him away from the house and down towards the harbour. He appeared in front of her again and she was forced to skirt around him. Walking through a ghast was not something you did, even if that ghast happened to be your best friend.

'You're going after the whalebone cithara, aren't you?'

She didn't reply.

'Because Bard told you to?'

'Granny said so too.'

'I was there, Oran. She said no such thing.'

'She said someone should bring it back!'

'Someone. Not *you*, specifically.'

'Well, no one else is doing anything to help, are they?'

He was quiet for a few paces, and then stopped at the top of the cliff path.

'I know what you're thinking,' he said.

She stopped too. The lighthouse lit the breaking waves the colour of rust, and beyond that sea and sky were all part of the same darkness. She turned to him. He was so faint he looked like watered-down milk. 'Do you? And what's that, then?'

'You want to play it yourself.'

Oran didn't reply at first, and that pause was all it took to show him he was right. 'I do not,' she lied.

'You can say that to yourself as much as you like, but I know you, Oran. I know exactly what's in your head. You think you're going to play your magic cithara and put everything right, and everyone will applaud you, and all over the Four Seas people will write songs about you—'

'That's not true!'

It was, in fact, true.

'Listen to me. This is not one of your usual adventures. It is not the same as sailing to Tusk, or fishing for giant squid, or searching for the Eye of the Harr. It is far, far more dangerous. And there is far, far more at stake. Please trust me.'

'Do you know what's more dangerous?' she said, putting her hands on her hips. 'Staying here. Doing nothing. Waiting for the ghasts and the grown-ups to finish talking. *That's* what's dangerous. For everyone. That's how the Duchess will get what she wants. Look at you, Alick. You're only half here! You've only been a day without music. You'll be gone for good before everyone else makes up their minds.'

Alick considered this for a moment. 'If you stay, then, yes, perhaps that's the end for me. But if you go, then it's the end for both of us. Little Drum couldn't bear it. Your maw couldn't bear it.' He paused. 'I couldn't bear it.'

'Why are you so sure I'm going to fail? I can handle the *Urchin*. I know the way. I've got a map, and it's only a few days' sailing.'

'The journey is only half of the danger, Oran. I'm more worried about the whalebone cithara itself. It's not yours to play. Not Bard's, either. Not anyone's. It belongs in the Great Barrow.'

'I'll bring it back to the Great Barrow.'

'After you've played it for the Duchess?'

'*Someone's* got to, haven't they?'

They stared at each other. The wind scoured the clifftops, and the waves boomed and hissed below them.

'I'm not going to change your mind, am I?' said Alick.

'No. Not unless you've got a better plan. How else are we going to get the Duchess to listen?'

'Honestly, Oran. You're stubborn as a limpet once you get an idea in your head.'

'Well, I learnt from the best,' she said with an ironical smile.

'Wait here,' said Alick.

He disappeared. Oran was left alone on the cliff, listening to the waves breaking below her. She felt very small, all of a sudden. The cold crept in amongst her skein and her sweater and she began to wonder whether this really was a good idea after all. Just when it seemed Alick had abandoned her completely, he reappeared with a long, musical sigh.

'Fine,' he said.

'Fine?'

Another long pause, the endless pulse of the sea.

'You can go. But I'm coming with you.'

It was hardly the most inspiring call to arms, but Alick's words were like a fair wind at Oran's back.

'Really?'

'You'll have to fetch me from the Great Barrow.'

'I can do that.'

'And I want to be somewhere safe and dry in the boat.'

'Of course. I'll look after you. It'll be just like old times!'

'I sincerely hope not.'

'You can be my navigator. If there's anyone who can stop me sailing off the edge of the sea, it's you.'

'I suppose.'

She grinned. Strange, she thought, that she should take so much courage from someone who typically had so little. His timid hope moved her far more than her own, slightly wild determination.

She stood up straight. Enjoyed her tallness for a moment.

'All right,' she said. 'Show me the way.'

⇒10⇐

The Great Barrow emerged from the earth like a breaching whale, dark and immense. The centre of the dome was a hundred feet high, and the stones that stood around its circumference were not much smaller. Nine of them, one for each member of the Chorus, the giants who had sung the world into being. In the light of the waning moon it was easy to think of them as the giants themselves, hulking, ageless, guarding the Barrow until the sea swallowed the island and their watch was ended. Under the dome, a thousand generations of islanders, with room for at least a thousand more.

'It's dark inside,' said Alick. 'Easy to get lost. Stay close to me, please.'

Oran walked up the hill and stood on the threshold of the Barrow. A huge, smooth slab of granite lay beneath her feet like a doormat. The moon illuminated carvings of the Chorus around the arch, each one represented by one of the nine birth instruments: cithara, fiddle, barrow fiddle, seahorn, bombard, reed pipe, bagpipes, bodhrán, handpan. Who knew how long those runes had been there? Not even the ghasts did.

Without her cithara on her back, Oran felt weightless and untethered. She rolled her shoulders, expecting to feel the tug of the straps, the rattle of the instrument. Trespassing in the Great Barrow felt wrong enough; trespassing without an instrument was unthinkable.

The cithara design was carved into the keystone of the arch. The first of all nine instruments, according to the myth. She traced it with her long fingers, took a deep breath and stepped over the threshold.

The inside of the Great Barrow was a labyrinth of pitch-black tunnels, lit only by the apparition of Alick. She had been here only once before, for Alick's funeral. At all other times, entering the tunnels was forbidden.

From somewhere below her, she thought, she could hear a choir of ghost voices. It was as though the earth itself was singing.

'What is that?' said Oran.

'That's the Moot.'

'It's still going on?'

'They reconvened when I told you that we were going to make the journey ourselves.'

'You *told* them?'

'Of course. No one's going looking for the whale-bone cithara without the ghosts knowing about it.'

It was not a comfortable thought. Oran had assured Bard that she would keep the whole business a secret. But now the secret was out and slipping away from her in all directions.

A little way in, Alick's glow began to show alcoves in the sides of the tunnel: the final resting places of the residents of Little Drum. Each was a small shrine, cut into the granite, and inside was placed the urn containing the islander's ashes and their skein. Their birth instrument was hung above both.

She followed him only a short way into the Barrow, using him like a lantern. He stopped sooner than expected.

'Here,' said Alick. He pointed to one of the smaller alcoves.

Oran hadn't seen his birth instrument since he'd

been alive. A barrow fiddle – larger than a normal fiddle, its tone deep and brooding. It was made of eelwood, that strange, dark, leafless tree that grew beneath the sea. It suited Alick's gloomy disposition perfectly.

'You're sure you want to do this?' she asked.

'I *don't* want to do this,' said Alick. 'But we don't have a choice. Someone's got to look after you.'

'We'll look after each other. Like always.'

'The score currently is twenty-two to zero,' said Alick. 'You've got a fair amount of catching up to do.'

'Fifteen to zero,' she said, and turned back to the shrine. 'All right. Ready?'

'I suppose.'

She lifted the urn – inscribed with the hearth song that she herself had composed for her friend – and stowed it in the bag with her provisions.

She looked at Alick. 'How do you feel?'

He looked down at himself, frowning. 'A bit strange. Wobbly. Like I'm on the deck of a ship.'

'Good practice for when we get out on the open sea.'

'That's not funny,' he said. 'I don't want to *think* about it.'

Oran hardly wanted to think about it, either. The joke barely concealed her anxiety. The responsibility of looking after her friend's ashes was enormous. A ghast could not stray from where his or her ashes were laid to rest, so she had to take them with her – but if she was to lose them, Alick would be gone for good, no matter how much she sang his hearth song. In fact, come to think of it, she'd never even heard of someone removing an ancestor's ashes from the island.

'Come on,' said Alick. 'Before I change my mind.'

Oran turned to leave and heard the choir of ghasts singing again. It wasn't the usual songs that drifted from the Great Barrow. It was a strange music, rather like the kind that Bard sang, the kind that touched your heart before your ears. The Old Music.

'Do you think we should go and see the Moot before we leave?' she suggested.

'No,' said Alick.

'But—'

'*No*,' said Alick again, more forcefully than Oran was expecting. 'We wouldn't have time even if it was allowed. Do you know how deep the Barrow goes?'

She shook her head.

'Well, it's deep. Very deep. We wouldn't make it back before morning.'

That only made Oran want to explore more. But Alick was already on his way out, leaving Oran in total darkness. She ran to catch him up.

When they reached the harbour it was, predictably, silent. The Headlanders' ships were cluttering the furthest end of the quay, under the lighthouse. Nobody on deck. The pier where Oran had tied up the *Urchin* was lost in darkness. It seemed to disappear off the edge of the earth.

They crept forward from among the nets and buoys. Alick dimmed almost to nothingness, a faint sketch of a boy on night's canvas. Together they crossed the boardwalk, Oran counting the posts until she reached her boat. She drew comfort from the smells of tar and seaweed.

They reached the *Urchin* and Oran leapt in. She put the bag containing her food and Alick's ashes under the seat at the front of the boat, made it snug. She tucked the dried sea-lettuce map under her skein.

'Happy?' she said.

'Delighted,' said Alick.

Oran laughed. 'See. Just like old times.'

She untied the rope and levered them away from the pier. Alick floated to the front of the boat and stood on the prow like a figurehead. A talisman. She was glad to have him with her.

'Are you sure you want to be up there?' she said.

'Quite sure. If I just look ahead I can forget I'm on a boat at all.'

Once they were in open water, Oran turned her gaze to the heavens. She scanned the constellations, found the Seahorse, followed its tail to the Bow and the Trident. She put up the mast and swung the boat around to face east. Lighthouse, harbour and home disappeared.

She looked at the rough map that Bard had drawn for her. All being well, she would be at the Spit by midday tomorrow, then Fiddlehead before nightfall. Then, with an early start, she could be at the Headland by the evening of the following day.

And after that? The crossing was only the start. She'd have to find a way to get into the Court and take the whalebone cithara without anyone seeing her. And if she found it, there was still the question of what she would do next. She'd promised Bard she would bring it straight back to Tusk, but then, if she was already at the Court, she may as well play it for the Duchess there and then. That was surely the best thing to do. Wasn't it?

She noticed Alick looking at her, as though reading her thoughts.

Down came the sail. The wind sang in the rigging, and the waves clapped against the hull. Oran listened to it all, as Bard had taught her, finding the rhythms and the melodies of the moments that passed her. The *Urchin* forged ahead into the vast emptiness of the sea, making a music all of its own.

⇒11⇐

They sailed through the night. The air was cool but not uncomfortable. Oran followed the stars until they were concealed by clouds, and then kept the prow of the boat straight, in the direction she thought was east.

Dawn had still not yet broken when Alick pointed out a row of lights on the horizon.

'Look!' he said. 'That must be the Spit. We're making good time. Maybe I *am* a good navigator.'

'You haven't done any navigating yet,' said Oran.

Whereas Little Drum was rocky and sheer, the Spit

was long and low and sandy, and the lamps of its villages were strung out neatly where the water met the sky. It was larger than Little Drum too. Her da had told her that the island nearly doubled in size at low tide, when the sea revealed its many miles of beaches. She was glad the landing would be easy, with no hidden reefs like Tusk or the Five Fingers.

The sky lightened slightly, but the sun still seemed reluctant to show its face. Oran began to feel desperately tired. Her argument with her maw, the loss of her cithara, her descent into the Barrow – it had all taken its toll. She ate some crackers and swigged some of the torc milk she'd decanted into her da's old hipflask. It made her feel a little stronger, but also a little homesick.

'What's wrong?' said Alick, with his uncanny knack for reading her mind.

'Nothing,' she said. 'Just tired.'

'You can sleep on the Spit. A quick nap won't do us any harm, seeing as we're ahead of schedule.'

He was right. They were making extraordinarily good time. Perhaps she'd send her parents a letter too. Just to put their minds at rest. Or would that make them worry more?

The lights of the villages were very close now, though the houses themselves were nowhere to be seen. A mist had risen from the sea. Nothing as thick as the Harr, but still enough to cling to Oran's lips and clothes and conceal the land ahead.

'Where is it?' Alick said quietly.

'Where's what?'

'The island. I can see the lights but I can't see the beach.'

'It's just this mist,' said Oran, trying to sound more confident than she was. 'It'll be there, don't worry.'

When the lamps ahead of her began to move, bobbing further apart, bobbing closer together, she understood what had happened; understood what was going to happen too. Her knuckles went white on the tiller. Her insides felt cold and briny.

'Oh dear,' said Alick.

The lights went out.

Her boat struck something hard and a sharp corner of rock smashed through the *Urchin*'s thick hull. Oran was thrown completely clear of the bench and fell face first into the seawater already flooding the bows. Her head rang with a sound like a struck bell, painfully loud, enough to make her eyes ache.

The boat sank with frightening speed. She grabbed Alick's ashes and climbed up on to the tiller, while the prow disappeared underwater. She could still hear the ringing, impossibly loud, and underneath it a thrashing, a gasping, a clattering like bones being shaken in a bag. She knew that she had only moments before she lost a leg, or an arm, or whatever part of her body was unlucky enough to be dangling in the water.

'Oran! Up here!'

Alick was above her, extending a hand that was no more use to her than thin air. Only the tiller and the top half of the mast were still above the waves now. She stood on the edge of the boat and leapt on to the same rocks that had sunk her.

Behind her a gigantic mouth emerged from the black sea. It was a bone-white, sharp-toothed grin with two spherical, transparent eyes at each corner. Above it, hanging from what looked like a long fishing rod, was the wispfish's distinctive lantern which it used to lure its prey on to the rocks. A second rod appeared and between them the two wispfish devoured Oran's boat in a few mouthfuls. A third snapped at her heels. She scrambled up the wet rocks, and when she was clear of their teeth she threw her provisions into the water. They gobbled them up, unappeased, and continued to thrash below her. Their dimmed lanterns protruded five or six feet from the surface of the water, level with Oran's face.

She stood with Alick and watched them circling. Oran had seen a wispfish washed up on the beach once, and it had terrified her then. The unsettling thing was that they looked the same whether they were alive or dead. Their skin, like their eyes, was completely transparent. From where Oran was perched, she seemed surrounded by a dozen eel-like skeletons, luminous against the darkness of the sea.

The clear, glassy tone was still reverberating all through her. It wasn't just from where she had hit her head. It was coming from the rocks around them.

'Can you hear that too?' she said.

Alick nodded. 'I thought it was just me.'

'Feels like I'm going deaf.'

'What is it?'

She shook her head.

Neither spoke for a while. There was no need to point out how disastrous their situation was. Words could hardly have done it justice, anyway.

The first rays of daylight banished the wispfish to the depths and sent the mist on its way. A pair of shadows fell over them where they sat and stretched into the waves in front of them. Oran turned to look into the sunrise and saw where she was properly for the first time. Two stacks of rock protruding from the sea, barnacled at their base but bare and weathered smooth above.

'I don't believe it,' she said. 'We've hit the Tuning Rock.'

On the first day of every new year, the islanders of Little Drum and Great Drum and a few other islands sent flotillas of boats out to the Tuning Rock. Here they struck the island with a ceremonial beater and tuned all their instruments to its single note. Oran had never been so close to it. At the new year ceremony, one strike was loud enough to be heard by thousands of musicians and rang out over the sea for hours afterwards.

'But that means we've gone north!' said Alick. 'We're a hundred leagues off-course!'

'Thank you, navigator . . .'

'Don't blame me, Oran. You got fooled by the lights too.'

'Well, at least we know where we are.'

'We are *marooned*. Whether you know the place or not doesn't really matter.'

Oran climbed carefully over the reef until she was next to one of the polished columns. Nobody knew how the Tuning Rock produced its note. Some said it was hollow and had been built that way. Others, Granny included, believed that it contained the spirit of a sea nymph. Oran flicked it lightly with one finger. It rang out louder than the bells of the town hall.

'It's amazing,' she said.

'It's a bit loud,' said Alick.

She wrapped her arms around Alick's urn and stared out over the grey-green sea. Hours passed. Ships passed too, but on the horizon, much too far away to hear or see them. She tried singing Alick's hearth song, but even that barely cheered them. It just reminded her of how much she missed her instrument, how much she missed her home. She pictured her maw and da sitting in their silent cottage, wondering where she was.

At midday — when she'd planned to be almost halfway to the Court — a boat came scudding past the rock within earshot. A frigate, and very old by the looks of things, but with immaculate sails patterned with a skein of purple, crimson and gold. Oran yelped when she saw it. There was only one group of musicians who were so ostentatious, who heralded their arrival with such pomp. She turned to Alick and grinned.

They exclaimed at exactly the same time: 'The Opera!'

Oran shouted until her lungs were raw and empty. Alick sent them his strange, glassy call on the breezes. The captain of the frigate peered at them both, but longer at Alick. For a moment Oran thought they might ignore her — the Opera were famously, fiercely suspicious of outsiders — but the captain spun the wheel and brought the ship up alongside the Tuning Rock.

'Ahoy there!' she called to Oran. Her accent had the southern burr of the Five Fingers. Ring, or Middle perhaps. 'You got an island all to yourself,' said the captain, laughing. 'You must be important!'

Some of the other musicians came up on deck and stared at Alick. They were flamboyantly dressed in silks and velvets, the same colour as their ship's sails: red, purple and gold. The women had their hair woven into complex plaits, the men's moustaches were waxed and curled. There was a proliferation of false teeth among them, made of gold, silver, ruby: sometimes all three in one mouth.

Alick got embarrassed and hid behind one of the prongs of the Tuning Rock.

'The wispfish wrecked my boat,' said Oran.

'So I see,' said the captain, and folded her arms.

The Opera's boat creaked in the silence. This was not going to be as easy as Oran had hoped.

'Do you think we could come aboard?' she said.

The captain sucked her teeth.

'I don't know about that, girl,' she said. 'You seem ill-starred to me. You've already caused one shipwreck – we don't need any more bad luck after the journey we've had. If there was something you could offer us, of course, that might change things.'

'A song,' said Oran. 'I can teach you a song.'

The crew didn't try very hard to hold in their laughter.

'Not likely,' said the captain.

'What do you mean?'

'We are the Opera! There's not a song in the Four Seas we don't know. Besides, my wee minnow, don't know how you'll teach anything without an instrument.'

Oran's face grew hot, with grief for her cithara, and anger at being called a 'minnow'. She opened her mouth to answer back, but there were no words there.

While she tried to think of a reason why the captain should take them aboard, the rest of the Opera had started pointing and muttering – not at Oran, but at a spot somewhere behind her. One of them walked along the gunwale to the captain and whispered in her ear.

She frowned and unfolded her arms. 'Now there's something you don't see every day.'

Oran turned to where Alick was skulking around the rocks. 'That's my friend, Alick,' she said.

'He's a ghost, is he not?'

Oran nodded.

'A useful friend to have.'

'Useful?'

'Does he speak?'

'Yes. He's just shy.'

'And he'll come with you, if we bring you on board?' said the captain.

'As long as I keep his urn safe,' said Oran, and lifted up Alick's ashes to show them.

More whispering between the captain and the man who Oran assumed was the first mate. Without another word, the captain spun the wheel and manoeuvred the frigate over to the rocks. She handled the ship as if it was no bigger than the *Urchin*.

'Come on then,' she hollered from the helm.

'Really?'

'I insist,' said the captain.

The ship still bobbed a good ten feet away from them, unable to get any closer because of the reef. Oran looked doubtfully down to the churning water. One of her boat's oars was still floating there, covered in teeth marks.

'Toss the urn across first,' said the first mate. 'Then you can paddle over yourself. Easy as that.'

She looked doubtfully at the urn. Alick suddenly appeared at her shoulder.

'No,' he said. 'You're not *tossing* anything.'

'I know, I know,' said Oran. 'I'll have to swim with you.'

'I don't think that's a good idea.'

'I don't know what else I can do, Alick.'

'What did she mean when she said I was *useful*?'

'I don't know,' said Oran. It was troubling. But she was hardly going to turn down the offer of being rescued by the *Opera* of all people.

The captain seemed to be getting impatient. She

shouted over to them, 'You coming aboard or aren't you? Come on. Quick sharp. Tides wait for no man, and no ghast, neither. You be careful with those ashes now, girl.'

Oran looked at Alick. His face was a portrait of worry. 'Seems the captain's more interested in you than me,' she said, trying to reassure him. 'You've saved us again. That puts the score at sixteen, I reckon.'

'Twenty-three,' he said miserably. 'Let's just get this over with.'

She wrapped his urn in her skein and clambered down the rocks. She looked into dark froth, then back at Alick. 'Ready?' she said.

He closed his eyes and held his nose, for reasons she didn't understand. He nodded.

Oran held the urn above her head and slipped into the icy breakers.

⇒12⇐

The Opera hauled them aboard like the catch of the day and dumped them on the deck. Oran sat and shivered and examined Alick's urn. It seemed intact. One of the crew brought her a dry shawl, another brought her a flask of something fiery. They didn't know what to do with Alick. They nodded and waved and one of them tried to shake his hand. It seemed they hadn't been in the presence of a ghast before.

'Well, this worked out all right, didn't it?' said Oran.

'In what way is any of this all right?' He sneezed, flew apart, came back together again.

'We're safer than we were on the *Urchin*, aren't we?' she said. 'We stand a far better chance of getting to the Headland on a boat like this. Perhaps we can ask them to take us to the Court?'

'Hmmm,' he said. He shivered in a way she hadn't seen before. Parts of him had become blurred. They looked like patches of mould.

'What's wrong?' Oran asked.

'I think some water got in the urn . . .'

The Opera's ship was under sail now and carving through the grey waves. The captain had handed the wheel to her quartermaster. She thumped down the stairs from the poop deck and pushed through the rest of the crew to where Oran was sitting at the base of mainmast.

'Hey-o! Back to work, you lazy lot!' she cried. 'The ship won't sail herself. And if you aren't manning your post, you got rehearsing to do!'

Some went about their duties, other gathered in the corners of the deck to practise. Oran looked on with envy as they set about polishing and tuning their instruments. They weren't the instruments of the Chorus. These men and women were southerners, and carried shining brass trumpets, trombones, tubas, and guitars of four, six and ten strings. The sound was bright and exotic and thrilling.

The captain stood in front of Oran, hands on hips, legs a little wider than they should have been. She gave a wide, bejewelled smile. 'Where've you washed up from, then?' she said. Even when she wasn't yelling at her crew her voice was incredibly loud. The Opera were actors as well as singers, so perhaps this was to be expected.

'Little Drum,' Oran said. She took off the shawl and proudly showed her skein.

'Long way from home.'

'So are you.'

'We are the Opera. The stage is our home – north, south, east or west. Though, to tell the truth, I can count the places where the Opera is welcome on one hand now. And I mean my *right* hand.' She raised it, clinking with bracelets. It was missing two fingers. 'Where is it that you're going?'

'The Headland.'

The captain roared with laughter. 'You don't say. The *Headland*! Off to the Court, no doubt, with all the other lords and ladies?'

'That's right.'

The woman's face froze for a moment, then she doubled over laughing again. 'You'll fit right in here, girl,' she said, 'patter like that! Ha ha!'

'It's not a joke,' said Oran. She flushed, partly

because she was worried that the captain's reaction was completely right. Maybe the whole thing *was* ridiculous.

The captain frowned, forgetting to close her mouth. A comical, theatrical mask of a frown. 'You're serious?'

Oran explained what had happened on Little Drum, about how the whole island had lost their instruments. She was on the verge of spilling everything about the whalebone cithara when she caught Alick's eye and realized that she had already said too much.

'And what? You're going to teach the Duchess a lesson?'

'I want to change her mind.'

'How exactly are you planning on getting through to the most stone-hearted woman in the Four Seas?'

'I'm going to sing for her.'

The captain narrowed her eyes. 'So, if I've understood correctly,' she said, 'you've set out across the open sea, the two of you, on your own, in a tiny little sloop, to confront the Red Duchess on her own doorstep?'

'I was planning on getting beyond the doorstep.'

The captain gave one last belly laugh. 'Well. By the squid that ate my father, if you two aren't the bravest buccaneers in all the Far Isles. I'd say you really do belong with us!'

Even Alick glowed when he heard that. Oran was quite sure he'd never been called brave in his life.

'Where are you going?' Oran asked. 'Is there any chance you could take us part of the way?'

'Part of the way?' said the captain. 'My dear, we can take you into the Duchess's bedchamber if you like.'

Oran and Alick looked at each other. 'What do you mean?'

'I mean you're in luck. For the first time in ten winters, the Opera are going back to Court.'

'Why? How? The Duchess will have you arrested as soon as she sees you!'

'Who says she's going to see us?' She winked at Alick and strolled away.

The Opera had visited Little Drum twice in Oran's lifetime. Oran had been nine years old when they'd last performed. She'd gone with Alick, a few months before he'd met his doom on the waves. It was a night she'd never forgotten: the glittering costumes, the colourful sets, the music that seemed at once so foreign and so familiar. She'd never seen fireworks before and hadn't seen them since. It had all been like a wonderful dream.

Not everyone had been happy to see them, though. There were many who thought of the Opera as little more than pirates who happened to play music – homeless, devious seafarers who arrived on the islands unannounced and unasked for. Whenever they paid a visit to one of the towns, their performances were invariably followed by fisticuffs, infidelities, and mysteriously vanishing valuables. Those who supported the Opera saw this as simply the price to pay for the show, because the players performed for free, and the shows were more lavish than anything on the Four Seas. Others resented the fact that they had no choice about when and where the Opera would descend. The Duchess was obviously in the latter camp.

Aged nine, Oran had decided she wanted to run away with them for a life of playing on the high seas. Now here she was. It had taken her five years, but the Opera's allure was undimmed.

The captain returned to upbraiding her crew and left her in the hands of the first mate, whose name was Guillam. He had a huge, red, curling moustache and a golden trumpet hanging from one shoulder. His face was slim, but he had a paunch that looked like a buoy concealed beneath his doublet.

'Do you have a name?'

'I'm Oran. This is Alick.'

'Right then, Oran,' he said. 'Something to eat, I think. And some warm clothes. If we've got anything in your size. Should have something somewhere but might be on the baggy side. We all live rather *heartily* aboard the *Overture*, if you know what I mean. I used to be a willowy young thing like you. Can you imagine that! I seem to be collecting ale down here' – he slapped his belly – 'and nowhere else. Never goes to my biceps, sadly. Ah well. Helps my playing, I say. You should see some of the guitar players. Can barely reach their instrument, it's so far away from them! Ha!'

Oran made an attempt at a laugh.

'And Alan,' he said, turning to Alick, 'what do you need? Have to admit, it's been a long time since I've seen a ghast. I remember an old man from the Green Sea who lived with the ghast of his mother. Just the two of them, in a shack he'd built on a lily pad. Wonderful singer, he was. Both of them were. You been to the Green Sea? Quite stunning! Can't see the water for a hundred leagues in any direction, with all the greenery. Lily pads the size of islands. Obviously that means you can't see what's *in* the water, either, and that's the dangerous thing. The captain here said she saw a leech that could swallow the ship whole. She likes a good a story though, so don't believe everything she says . . .'

He turned and walked away over the deck, never once looking back, never once pausing to take a breath. He talked and talked and talked, his diction strangely clipped and aristocratic. Alick looked completely overwhelmed.

'Are we meant to follow him?' he said.

Oran shrugged. 'I suppose so,' she said.

Guillam led them down into the belly of the frigate. The lower deck was gloomy, but drier and warmer than she'd expected. It smelled of sawdust and perfume and burning blubber. Each side of the deck was lined with hammocks, which Oran thought a little basic given the expensive tastes of the Opera, but they seemed comfortable enough. Two more members of the Opera were currently asleep in them and snoring.

Guillam prattled on. 'You'll have to slum it down here with the rest of us,' he said. 'No feather beds, I'm afraid, but you won't get tipped out of a hammock in a storm, and we've been through some absolute stinkers in the last few days. I thought the thunder was going to shake the teeth out of my mouth — and these are expensive teeth!'

'Where—'

'Sorry. Don't listen to me. Last thing you want to think about is storms when you've just escaped a shipwreck. What's wrong with you, Guillam?' He struck himself on the forehead. 'Weather seems to have cleared up, anyway, and besides, most of the hurricanes stay south this time of year, which you probably know. Or maybe you don't, coming from Little Drum? That's where you said you were from, didn't you?'

'Yes—'

'Never been there myself. New addition to the crew, you see. Would love to go. Ghasts all over the place, isn't that right? Well, you won't find any ancestors here. That's the thing about the Opera, tends to attract people who are trying to *escape* their past. I grew up on Harp myself, you can probably hear it in this silly accent of mine. I'd rather forget all about my family, and they'd rather forget all about me, so it's worked out nicely. Not that I have anything against ghasts in principle.'

'What—'

'Anyway, this food. Listen to me, going on and on, and your stomach rumbling away! Let me see what I can rustle up. Bit of food, mug of something warm. Have you ever tried spiced kelp juice? I know it doesn't sound all that appetizing, but it is *quite* delicious, I promise you. Anything else? Nothing for you, Alan? You're sure?'

'There is one thing, actually,' said Oran quickly, for fear she'd be cut off again.

'Say away, my dear,' said Guillam. 'Your wish is my command! Up to a point.'

'Well . . .' She looked at Alick. He was still looking

strangely blotchy. It had been a long time, she realized, since she'd sung anything for him. 'I was wondering if, maybe, you might have a spare cithara on board.'

Guillam's expression went from joy to misery, with nothing in between.

'I'm afraid we don't have any of your kind of instruments. I'm dreadfully sorry, Oran. What a horrible thing it must be, to lose one's lifelong companion like that.'

Just hearing him say it aloud brought a lump to Oran's throat, which she quickly swallowed. 'Do you have something similar? A guitar, maybe?'

Guillam's glittering smile returned without warning. 'Why, yes, I believe we do! I'm sure it is nothing like as beautiful as your own instrument, but it is very fine. Have you played the guitar before? It has ten strings, the one in question. How many strings does a cithara have? Doesn't matter. I'm sure you'll get along well with it. I'll dig it out. And the food. The food!'

He went through a door at the other end of the deck and could be heard puffing and panting and shifting boxes. When he returned he was holding a guitar under one arm and a whole roast chicken under the other. He set the chicken down on the floor without a plate, and handed the guitar to Oran.

She looked it over. It was made of a very pale

wood, almost white. Its body was thin and its neck was very long. A good fit for her. 'Who did it belong to?' she asked.

'Nobody,' said Guillam. 'It's just a spare we have. Instruments get broken with all the moving and packing we do.'

She rubbed her hands over the varnish and looked up at Alick. Guillam watched her, his mouth slightly open in anticipation.

'Could we be alone for a moment?'

Another sea change on Guillam's face. 'Oh goodness, of course you can. Stupid man!' He rubbed his face vigorously. 'Here I am, talking and talking and talking and you just want to collect yourself. A thousand apologies.'

'Please, don't apologize, you've been very kind.'

'Say no more. Guillam shall away.' He bowed and climbed back up to the top deck.

Holding the guitar felt very strange. The position of her plucking hand was the same if she held the instrument upright, but it had three more strings than her cithara, and the steel frets were painful under her fingers. The body felt cumbersome. But besides all of that, there was an underlying discomfort of betrayal: the feeling that she had abandoned an old friend.

'Can you play it?' asked Alick.

'I suppose we'll find out.'

She tentatively struck one of the strings. The sound was different from what she was used to – not worse, or better, just different in quality. Woody in the bottom, bright and metallic at the top.

It only took her a few attempts at Alick's hearth song for her to get to grips with the fingering on the guitar's neck. She felt pleased with herself for that. How many other people were there in the world who could learn a new instrument so quickly? Then she heard her mother's voice, again, telling her not to get too big for her boots.

Oran played until her fingertips were throbbing. Alick joined in. They sang of his birth – he'd been born in the middle of the Harr, while his parents had been lost on a clifftop – of his upbringing. Of his qualities, his loyalty, his love, his hardworking nature. Of the time he built the largest sandcastle the islanders had ever seen. The song contained all his triumphs and his failures, unflinching, unsentimental, right down to the day he died.

O cursed Harr, so full of spite,
To hide the sun, turn day to night!
For lost with neither oar nor sail,
Brave Alick's sight was bound to fail;
And on that mazy ocean black
The fog that bore him snatched him back.

He turned the colour of rose gold, his features becoming brighter, more distinct, until he outshone the blubber lamps.

When they stopped, Oran noticed that the snoring had stopped along with them. The two members of the Opera were sitting up in their hammocks, open-mouthed. Guillam was standing at the bottom of the steps, along with half a dozen of the other players. The captain was in front of them, her hands clasped together.

'My, oh my,' she said, shaking her head in wonder. 'A useful pair indeed.'

'Sorry,' muttered Oran. 'I'm out of practice.'

'Out of practice? I swear, by the clam that took my fingers, I have *never* heard anything like it.' She stepped forward. 'Well, that settles it. You've got no choice now. Wouldn't you agree, Guillam?'

'No choice at all,' said Guillam, spreading his hands in a helpless gesture. 'Sorry!'

'Choice?' said Oran.

'You must join us. As an honorary member of the Opera.'

⇌13⇌

Life in the Opera wasn't as romantic as the nine-year-old Oran had thought. As soon as she'd been welcomed into their company, with hugs and slaps on the back and many more swigs of tongue-blistering kelp juice, the captain put her to work.

'It's not all lounging around aboard the *Overture*, as much as Guillam would like it to be,' she said. Guillam spluttered in protest. 'A well-run ship is like a well-tuned orchestra. All different parts working in harmony.'

'What can we do?' asked Oran.

'Much as I like you, my girl, you'll start at the bottom. Deck needs a-scrubbin', and cannons need a-polishin'. Let's look our very best for Her High and Mightiness the Duchess.'

'What about me?' said Alick.

The captain inclined her head. 'If I might have the honour,' said the captain, 'you and I need to talk strategy.'

'Strategy?'

'Aye. Come with me please.'

She strode across the deck to the captain's cabin and Alick followed her, bewildered. He looked at Oran. Oran shrugged.

Guillam handed her a bucket and a brush and she set to work. It wasn't long before her back and shoulders were burning. Guillam joined her out of sympathy, on his hands and knees in all his finery, but made a half-hearted job of it. He kept stopping to tell her stories and ask her questions. He ate a lot too. He had an extraordinary variety of foods hidden in the folds and pockets of his doublet and cloak: cheeses, meats, dried fruit, sweet-rolls. At least two hipflasks, as well.

'Why's the captain talking to Alick?' she asked him.

'Well. Now I should probably let the captain tell you that.'

She looked behind at the captain's cabin, but the

windows were blank and she heard nothing from inside. Above it the quartermaster was leaning on the wheel. He caught her eye and grinned.

'Missed a bit,' he shouted.

Oran grumbled and went back to scrubbing.

'That song you were singing was a rare thing,' said Guillam. He blew a hair off the turkey leg he'd just found and took a bite. 'What was it?'

'His hearth song.'

'Hearth song?'

'It's the song of your ancestors. Everyone gets one composed for them when they pass over.'

'Aha!' He pointed the half-eaten drumstick at her. 'The High Music!'

Oran stopped and sat up. 'The what?'

'The High Music. That's what we called it on Harp. High Music was the serious, complicated stuff composed for our important ancestors. We were only allowed to play it in the Mausoleum. I can still remember some of the funeral dirges now.'

He put his trumpet to his lips and played a series of long, low notes. He hadn't even warmed up but his tone was exquisite – more like a human voice than a brass instrument. Some of the crew looked at him. Some joined in. He nodded appreciatively.

'It's beautiful,' said Oran. 'And very sad.'

'And *boring*,' Guillam added. 'The Low Music was

what I liked. The shanties and the ballads and the dances. That was most of the reason for the split between me and my dear family. Too much of a commoner for them!' He tore off another bit of turkey and spoke with a full mouth. 'But here's the *fascinating* thing, Oran: your lovely song was High Music that sounded like Low Music. The perfect kind, as far as I'm concerned!'

'We don't really think of songs as high or low back home,' said Oran. 'Anyone is allowed to play anything. They're encouraged to, actually. Or at least, they were.' She felt another pang of homesickness, which was then matched by a sharp pain in her finger. 'Ouch!' She lifted her hand to see a ragged splinter protruding from the tip. She picked it out, hissing.

'That'll do,' said Guillam. 'We don't want you ruining your playing hand just because the captain wants a nice clean ship.'

'What's the captain's name?' asked Oran, sucking the blood from her fingertip.

Guillam thought for a moment. 'You know what, I've never thought to ask. We all just call her "Captain". Want to see the gun deck?'

He didn't wait for her reply but heaved himself up from where he was sitting and led her to the steps in the forecastle. The gun deck was one above the crew's quarters. The dark, blunt shapes of the cannons crouched in rows. Oran put her hand on the brass of the one nearest her, felt its coldness, its immovable weight. In the corners were piles of cannonballs, black and shining like huge fish eggs. The smell of gunpowder stung her nostrils.

'Beauties, aren't they?' said Guillam. 'Eight-pounders, the lot of them. Picked them up in the south, and by goodness we needed them!'

'What for?'

'The Green Sea's a lawless place. And audiences aren't as . . . appreciative as up here.'

Oran stepped away from the fuse with an irrational feeling that it might explode at any moment. 'Will you be using them when we reach the Headland?'

'That depends how well things go. Perhaps we will. Fancy a go? They're rather fun!'

'I'm not sure I want to.'

'You might have to, if it comes down to it.'

Oran suddenly felt a long way out of her depth. She turned and looked him in the eye. 'Please tell me why you're going to the Court. I think I should know, if I'm part of your crew.'

'It's hard to explain,' said Guillam. He hummed and tugged at the frills on his blouse, but was saved from his discomfort by the arrival of Alick and the captain. Alick, as ever, looked worried.

'At ease, Guillam,' the captain said. 'There's no

explaining to be done.'

'No?'

'I've just had an interesting chat with our ghast friend here. Seems we're going to the Court for exactly the same reason as young Oran is.'

They sat in the captain's cabin around a gigantic map of the Four Seas. Oran had never seen the world drawn out in such detail. It was so much larger than she'd ever imagined, and there was even more to explore off the map's edges. In one corner she had placed the scrap of sea lettuce on which Bard had sketched her plan of the palace. It looked like a child's drawing by comparison, and Oran couldn't help feeling embarrassed.

The cabin was crammed with curiosities gathered or stolen from the Opera's travels – gold and silver-ware, horns, guitars, accordions, skeins of unfamiliar design, brightly coloured stones and corals, fossilized eggs, tusks and bones. Above the map swung a puffer-fish as big as the table itself, dried and hollow like a spiny gourd.

The captain had put on a magnificent cloak of galleon-bird feathers that shimmered turquoise in the light of the blubber lamps. Oran didn't know if this was one of the Opera's costumes or just what the captain liked to wear.

She marked out their route using the skull of a spindlebill. When she reached Stonefirth, the capital, she stuck the pointed beak into the table and it stayed there quivering.

'We're not welcome on Harp or the Horns or any of the Near Isles,' she said. 'The Duchess's navy will be in their waters too. We'll have to get to Stonefirth via the back door, and that means crossing the Great Gulch.'

Oran felt a shudder of something between fear and excitement. The Great Gulch was the ancient trench that lay between the Far and Near Isles. That was where the Greymers were rumoured to live.

'Once we're ashore, that's where you two can really change the game. Oran, we've got your lovely map of the Court; and Alick, we've got you to scout things out.' She laughed. 'Everything's so much easier when you can walk through walls!'

Alick glimmered uncertainly.

Oran cleared her throat. 'If we're both looking for the whalebone cithara,' she said quietly, 'then who's going to keep it when we find it?'

The captain's face creased in confusion. 'The what-what cithara?'

'The whalebone cithara,' said Oran. 'I thought you said we were both looking for the same thing?'

'Oh no,' said the captain. 'We're not after one

instrument in particular. We're going for the whole lot.'

'*All* of them?'

The captain nodded. 'We're going to clean the woman out! Take everything she has. I'm sure we can gift you one instrument, if that's what you want. What's so special about this whalebone cithara anyway?'

Oran could feel Alick's eyes on her.

'It's sort of an heirloom,' she said.

'Oh aye, plenty of those in the Duchess's collection,' said the captain. 'What's so special about it?'

Oran didn't want to say too much. 'It just has a very special tone. The sort of tone that makes people listen.'

'I see. And you're planning on playing it for the Duchess? All on your own? Right there in the Court?'

Again, Oran fought against the undertow of her own pride. Her promise to Bard was a distant echo.

'Maybe,' she said.

Alick tutted.

'Well,' said the captain, 'that's mighty bold of you. Of course, I've always said that a soloist is only as good as the musicians who she's playing with. But if there's anyone in the world who can charm the Duchess with a song, I'd say it's you.'

'What are you going to do with the other instruments?' Oran asked. 'Sell them?'

'Sea's teeth, no!' said Guillam. 'The Duchess has the finest collection of instruments in all of the Four Seas. Rare and beautiful pieces, all of them. We'd never exchange them for something as useless as gold. They need *playing* – the Duchess just has them cooped up in that palace gathering dust.'

'I still don't understand why she'd collect them in a museum,' Oran said.

'Because she's a monster.'

'No, I mean, I don't understand why she'd want to keep them at all. If she hates music so much, why doesn't she destroy them?'

'Don't ask me how her mind works. She's a madwoman. You know the song, Oran. You're talking about someone who *murdered* her whole family not much more than a year ago, just so she didn't have to share power! Parents, sister, husband. The lot.'

'I know that's what the song says, but that doesn't necessarily make it true . . .'

The captain raised an eyebrow. 'You sound like you're defending her.'

'I'm not defending her.' Then what was she saying? 'I don't know. I just remember, when she came to Little Drum, she wasn't what I expected. She seemed sad.'

'Pah! Then she's already won. Don't you go feeling sorry for her, lassie. She isn't called the Red Duchess for nothing. She's got blood up to her elbows. And you're a braver woman than I for confronting her. I just hope your special cithara is all it's cracked up to be.'

⇒14⇐

After the meeting in the cabin the wind picked up and the captain needed another pair of arms on the halyard, so Oran was relieved from her deck-scrubbing duties. From there she was shown the ropes of the mizzen mast and the bowsprit. She desperately wanted to be alone with Alick for a moment, to talk, but he was sent up to the crow's nest to be lookout. It made sense since, unlike everyone else, there was no chance of him falling to his death from the top of the mast. He seemed rather proud to be given the honour.

When night fell and the work lessened, there was

more to be learnt. The Opera were keen to make her one of their own. She learnt chess. She learnt the trumpet. She learnt the strange, complex dances of the southern islands, though she felt tall and clumsy around the captain, who had appointed herself Oran's tutor. She learnt some rude shanties, and taught some too.

She learnt that cake and cheese and kelp juice do not mix well.

Past midnight she was lying in her hammock, clutching her belly. Alick was humming somewhere next to her. The rest of the Opera were still roaring and cavorting overhead. She heard the thumping of feet and some uncomplimentary lyrics about the Duchess and an amorous porpoise.

'How are you feeling?' said Alick.

Oran turned in her bunk. It lurched violently in one direction, her stomach in another. 'Like I've swallowed a nest of eels.'

'Not that. I mean, how do you feel about what we're doing?'

She was quiet a moment. Her thoughts swilled around her head like ale in a barrel. 'I don't really know. None of it seems real while we're out here in the middle of nowhere.'

'What about the pirates?'

'The Opera, Alick.'

'If you say so.'

'I like them,' she said, and then paused. 'But you're right. I'm not sure how happy I am about us teaming up. I feel like it'll be *more* rather than less dangerous if we try and break into the Court together.'

'Well, they are professional thieves,' said Alick. 'That's one good thing.'

'They're professional *musicians*, Alick.'

'Who steal things.'

The song above seemed to be quietening down now. There were groans and yawns and exhausted ebbs of laughter. Oran closed her eyes and tried to still her churning stomach. For a moment she felt herself slipping gratefully into sleep.

The thumping on the ship's timbers started up again. She groaned. 'Ach, I thought they'd finished dancing for the night.'

'Oran.'

'What?'

'It's not coming from up there.'

She looked at Alick. He'd taken on the shivering, frost-like aura that he got when he was scared.

She sat up and listened again. Three loud knocks, which she felt vibrate through the strings of the hammock. He was right. It came from beneath them. Something was hammering on the hull, from outside the ship.

'What is that?' said Alick.

Oran shook her head. The knocks came from fore and aft, clattering down the whole length of the ship. The blubber lamps shuddered on their chains, and where there had once been the quiet slap of the waves there was now a great hissing, as though something was dragging in the water to slow the frigate down. Footsteps overhead – not the drunken thunder of the Opera's dancing, but a quick, urgent patter.

Guillam came down the steps to the crew's quarters. His face was grave – a strange thing to see in place of his usual exaggerated smiling and scowling.

'I'm sorry to throw you both in at the deep end, as it were—'

Oran and Alick looked at each other.

'— but we may need your help. Bring your instrument.'

'My instrument? Why? What's happening?'

But he had already gone.

Oran grabbed the guitar that she had been playing earlier and walked unsteadily to the other end of the quarters. The *Overture* yawed and pitched, skidding left and right as much as she went forwards. Oran had to climb after Guillam on her hands and knees. The guitar banged clumsily on each step.

When she came out on deck it was raining, cold and hard as pebbles. The wind came from every direction and the *Overture*'s sails had been furled to keep them from being torn to shreds. Most of the Opera were standing at the gunwales, peering over the edge of the ship; some were hanging dangerously from the rigging. The captain was marching up and down with her accordion in her hands, the three fingers of her right hand drumming nervously on the keys. She saw Oran, came straight over to her and pulled her into a tight embrace.

'Listen, lassie,' she said, almost shouting over the wind's caterwauling, 'I'm sorry to foist this upon you so soon after joining us, but we may need you save our hides.'

Oran felt a new surge of nausea. 'Save your what?'

'There's something I need to do first, though.'

'What?'

'I would like to bestow upon you the position of captain of the *Overture*.' She placed her tricorn hat on Oran's head.

'*Captain?*'

'Do you accept this great honour?'

'I don't understand.'

'You've got the hat now, so it's basically a done deal.'

'But I don't want to be captain.'

The captain – now no longer the captain – gripped her shoulders and gave her a fierce look. 'Sea's teeth, just say *yes*.' Her fingers dug into the tops of Oran's arms.

'Yes. *Yes.* Ouch!'

'Thank you. Sorry.' The captain released her.

'Can you tell me what's going on? What was that sound? Why've we stopped?'

The woman looked around the ship, as though expecting to see someone jump aboard, but no one was moving. The clouds seemed inches above their heads, soot-black, and the rain came down in great ragged sheets. No moon, no stars.

'It's the Greymers.'

The name no longer filled Oran with excitement. The story and the reality were two very different things. She was cold and wet and terrified. And now, with a flash of anger, she realized why the captain had put her in charge. The Greymers always challenged the ship's captain to a contest in song.

'So it's up to me to save us all, is it? Well, that's fine leadership!'

'You're obviously the best player on board, Oran! Even on that old guitar.'

'I thought you said we'd get through the Gulch safely.'

'I thought we would. The sea was flat as a flounder. Then this storm came out of nowhere.'

'You know what?' said Oran. 'I think I *would* make

captain than you.'

The *Overture* pitched forwards, as though someone very heavy had sat on the bows.

Then they came aboard.

The first thing Oran saw was their arms, long and slender and weirdly jointless, like the arms of an octopus. They clutched at the rails and hauled themselves aboard, and for a moment stood perfectly still, watching the crew. Oran could smell something like fermented fish through the freshness of the rain.

From a distance they could have been men or women, but the closer they came odder they looked. In the half-light the Greymers' skin gleamed dully like old pewter, puckered and scarred with tooth marks. Their bellies swelled like pufferfish, while gills gaped beneath their armpits. Their mouths were thin and lipless and curved in an expression of constant displeasure.

More of the Greymers had climbed aboard the stern of the ship. They enclosed the crew in a circle, some standing around the mainmast, others perched behind on the poop deck. The Opera huddled in terror. Hardly the fierce sea dogs that Alick thought they were.

Alick? Where was he?

There arose a humming, a drone, but not totally without tune. Oran couldn't see any instruments, and it was a moment before she realized the tone was coming from the Greymers themselves. Their bodies inflated like bagpipes, and the wheezing sound escaped from the slits under their arms. They began to beat upon the deck with their feet. Each thump was accompanied by a squelch, and Oran saw green seawater seep from their legs on to the boards she'd spent so long cleaning.

The Greymer nearest her stepped forwards. He addressed himself to Oran, seeing the captain's hat perched upon her head. His mouth opened like a whale's, ribbed and cavernous. The voice had a strange gurgling quality to it, but it seemed to resonate through the whole ship into the sea.

His opening verse was accompanied by a blast of the fish stench that made her eyes water.

I once knew a girl with crow-black hair and a crow-black
*   heart in her chest;*
For she left her maw
On a silent shore
When her home was sorely oppressed.

The tune was very unusual, but it was the words that brought Oran up short. They were singing about *her*. The mention of her maw nearly had her choking, but she let his rebuke be fuel for her reply.

She drew a deep breath and sang, not without anger:

*Her heart was black with sorrow and fear, but the poor
    girl did no wrong;*
Through storms she fought
To the Duchess's Court
To save the Far Isles with a song.

She added a few flourishes on the guitar, making new harmonies with the Greymers' drone. This seemed to please her opponent. He sang again.

*She wasn't just heartless – thoughtless too – she sailed
    through waters forbidden.*
She forced her crew
'Cross the fathomless blue
Where the cunning Greymers lay hidden.

He was trying to goad her! She doubled the speed of her playing, adding notes and runs where there had once been space, and picked up where he left off:

*The Greymers were foolish to challenge the girl and
    think that the triumph was theirs*
For she'd practised hard
With the goddess-like Bard
And she banished them back to their lairs.

The Greymer had no eyebrows, but he raised the skin where his eyebrow should have been. Again that sly, superior smile.

> Her lessons meant nothing; a child of the land, she played
>   with the grace of a cow.
> Her fingers were slow
> And her words wouldn't flow
> And despairing she jumped from the prow.

Her fingers were slow, were they? She would give them this much: they knew how to get under her skin. She sank into that deeper place of listening, as Bard had taught her, a still pool in the midst of the storm. She heard the bass of the thunder, the trill of the wind, the percussion of the rain on the decking. She heard and played and wove it into the song, and suddenly the music was unfurling in directions that no one could have foreseen, not even herself, all counter-rhythms and strange extended chords. Just as when she had played for Magmalley, the song came from somewhere beyond thought. The sounds that came from her lips were not words, but nor were they without meaning.

When she looked up she realized that she was playing alone. The Greymers were staring at her, gills and inflated bellies pulsing. The storm had stopped. A shaft of moonlight fell upon the Greymers' skin and the beads of spray shone like hundreds of thousands of jewels.

Oran let go the neck of the guitar and the last echoes of the song descended on the ship as it rocked on the calmed sea.

'Forgive us,' said the Greymer. His speaking voice was thick and burbling, nothing like his singing. He bowed.

'For what?' said Oran, her whole body still vibrating from navel to fingertips.

'We cannot not compete with the Old Music.'

The Old Music? Was that what she had played?

'Well,' she said, 'you should have thought of that before you came on board.'

The rest of the Greymers began bowing too. Then they went lower, slithering around the deck on their hands and knees. 'Forgive us,' they said. 'Forgive us.'

Oran was too confused to reply. Most of her thoughts were still caught up in the song. She had got as far as parting her lips when the Greymers slunk back to the ship's gunwales, still prostrate, and then dived back into the sea.

⪢15⪡

As expected, the Opera cracked open the whisky well before breakfast. The sun had only just come up but they were already pouring themselves endless toasts.

'You are a wonder, my girl!' said the captain. 'Besting the Greymers! There's not a captain alive who's done such a thing! I've never heard anything like it. I could have sworn you stopped the storm itself with your singing.'

Oran had wondered that too. Hadn't Bard spoken of singing to the wind and the waves? But that was impossible – she was playing an old, second-hand guitar, not the whalebone cithara. She tried to keep her pride in check, but she couldn't stop thinking about what the Greymers had said. Why were they so apologetic? Why were they so haughty one minute, so grovelling the next? She needed to speak to Alick.

Where was he? She was already on her second tour of the ship, carried aloft on the Opera's shoulders, when she realized he still hadn't come up from below. She squirmed out of the crew's arms and looked up and down the deck.

'Have any of you seen Alick?'

They stopped their singing and cheering.

Guillam shrugged. 'He's hiding in the hold, isn't he?'

'He was,' said Oran. 'But I'm surprised he hasn't shown his face yet.'

'Well, tell him to come up! He needs to swear his allegiance to his new captain.'

The Opera went back to celebrating. They didn't seem particularly worried, but Oran could feel something was wrong. She hurried down the steps, past the gun deck, into the sleeping quarters. She looked at the piles of boxes and stacked barrels. Alick's urn wasn't where she'd left it.

'Alick?' she called. She thought she heard a reply. It may have been the creak of the timbers.

She searched among the hammocks, between the ship's great ribs, in the dark corners of the hold. She took a blubber lamp that was hanging on the wall and ventured into the hindmost section of the ship. It smelled of rot and bilge water. She found some old sails, badly folded and full of holes. Three boxes that had once contained dry crackers but were now mostly full of maggots. The dried carcass of a sea turtle that they apparently hadn't found a use for.

And there was Alick's urn. It must have rolled all the way back when the Greymers had dragged the ship to a halt. The lid was lying a few feet away. The urn itself was cracked in half and Alick's ashes lay in a mound among the pieces.

'Help . . .' said a voice.

'Alick! Hold on!'

Oran spun round with the lamp. She saw glimpses of him wherever she looked. A set of fingers, very faint; the suggestion of a mouth and nose; one eye and one miserable eyebrow. It was as though, with the urn broken, he wasn't able to hold himself together.

'I'm slipping . . .' he said. His voice was like wind over sand dunes.

Oran ran through the cargo hold looking for a cup, a box, any kind of vessel. There was nothing that was the right size. All the crates were far too big, and full of holes.

She leapt up the steps to the deck two at a time until she was back blinking in the daylight.

'Help!' she shouted. 'I need something that can hold ashes!'

The Opera looked at her, swaying, their skins full of whisky.

'What's that, Cap'n?' said the captain.

'A pot, a box. Something with a lid.' They frowned at her. 'Quickly!'

They looked around the ship and patted their pockets.

Guillam produced a small silver tin. 'I use this for keeping sweetroot in. I suppose I could part with it.'

Oran shook her head. 'Too small.'

There was a numbness in her arms and legs. In her head too, as though she wasn't seeing or hearing things properly. Of course she shouldn't have brought Alick out on the open sea. He hadn't wanted to come at all. She'd forced him, selfishly, like she always did, and now she'd lose him for ever.

'What about this?' said the captain. She'd produced a leather coin pouch from one of her sleeves. It looked big enough.

Oran snatched it without saying anything. She hurried back down to the hold. The thumping footsteps of the rest of the crew followed her.

In the damp and the dark she took cupped

handfuls of Alick's ashes and lifted them carefully into the leather bag. In went the pieces of the urn too. She stared at the spot where it had broken. It was obvious that some of the dust had found its way between the cracks in the wood and would never be retrieved.

She pulled the drawstring of the pouch closed and held it to her chest. She put out the lamp so she could see Alick better. The whole Opera stood behind her in total darkness.

The boy appeared slowly. At first he was indistinct, a swirl of sea foam, and then his features became clearer. He didn't wear an expression of any kind.

'Alick?' Oran whispered his name, as if to speak any louder would blow him away again. She squeezed the pouch of his remains tighter still, until she could feel her heart beating through it. 'Are you all right?'

His brow drooped. Oran couldn't help smiling at it. It was better than the strange, blank face he'd had until now.

'I feel awful,' he said weakly. 'Like a bottle of beer all shaken up.'

'I'm so sorry!' said Oran. 'I should have been looking after you.'

'I thought that was my job.'

Oran laughed, and tears came with it. 'That makes the score twenty-three to one,' she said. 'I'm catching you up.'

'Doesn't count,' said Alick. 'You can't abandon me, and then give yourself the credit for saving me.' He drifted around the hold, stretching his neck and arms and fingers experimentally. 'Am I all here?' he said.

'What do you mean?' said Oran, sniffing.

'Look at me. Is all of me here? I feel like I've . . . lost a bit of me.'

She looked him up and down. Made a circle around him. That was when she saw it. Or rather, didn't see it.

'Your ear . . .' she said.

'What about it?'

'It's not there.'

'Which one?'

'Left one.'

'Must have slipped through the timbers.'

The whole ship was quiet.

'Well,' he said, 'now I know which side to stand when I don't want to listen to you singing.'

After the run-in with the Greymers the ship felt lighter, somehow. The weather had improved too. When they eventually emerged from the hold, the sky was bright blue and enormous. The deck baked and shimmered under the hot sun.

'I'm going up to the crow's nest,' Alick announced once they were out of the hold.

'Don't you want to stay down here?'

'I never want to go in that hold ever again, thank you. I like it in the crow's nest. Fresh air. Nice and quiet. Besides, I'm still meant to be your navigator, aren't I? I've lost an ear, but I've still got both eyes.'

Oran felt a queasy mixture of pride and shame. She shouldn't have asked him to come. She should have taken better care of him. This really wasn't a place for a ghast. She could tell he wasn't feeling himself.

'All right, but I'm keeping you close from now on,' she said. She tied the bag of his ashes around her waist. 'There. Now there's no way we're getting separated.'

'You say that like it's a good thing,' said Alick, and drifted to the top of the mast.

Oran heard the captain stomping behind her, then felt a heavy hand on her shoulder. She turned and proffered the tricorn hat. The captain looked affronted.

'No, no,' she said, 'I won't have any of that. You've earned the title now. The crew are waiting for their orders.'

'But I have no idea how to captain a ship!'

'It's easy. You just tell everyone else what to do and stand impressively at the wheel a couple of times a day.'

Oran looked up at the helm. 'Well, I can do at least one of those things.'

'Be my guest,' said the captain – Oran would still think of her as that, no matter what she said.

She climbed the steps next to the captain's cabin. (Would she be allowed to sleep in there now? she thought. The captain's bed looked sumptuous . . .) It was the first time she'd been on the poop deck, and it was higher than expected. She saw down the full length of the *Overture*, and over the expanse of the Gulch. The sea was calm, but among the low waves she could see wide, grey-brown tracks.

'What are those?' Oran asked.

'Whelk roads,' said the captain.

'What are whelk roads?'

'Exactly what you'd think they'd be. The whelks go over the sea floor to feed at the Headland's estuary. Wherever they go they churn up the bottom, and everything floats to the top, leaving these helpful little routes. Bless the little blighters!'

'So we can just follow these to the Court?'

'Simple as that! So, over to you.'

Oran grasped the handles of the wheel, and found it spun more easily than she'd expected. She pulled to starboard and the *Overture* carved smoothly over to one of the mirrored roads.

'A natural!' shouted the captain.

Oran smiled, inside and out. Her heart seemed to fill her whole chest.

There was another full day's sailing ahead of them, but it passed quickly. In truth, Oran was only partly in charge of the ship. The captain didn't relinquish her duties as easily as she relinquished her hat, and still marched around the deck instructing the crew. Oran was glad for the help. They made an efficient trio. The captain watched the sails and the sailors, Alick kept his eyes on the sea, and Oran steered them, according to Alick's instructions, along the smooth path of the whelk road.

16

Late in the afternoon, the Headland appeared as a thick smudge between sea and sky. By sunset it filled all of the horizon.

'It's so big,' Oran said to the captain. 'I always thought the sea only had islands in it.'

'It is an island,' said the captain.

'Really?'

'Well, *all* land is an island, when you think about it. Any direction you walk in, you'll meet the sea eventually. We just haven't gone all the way around this one, yet.'

'Why not?'

'It's a *very* long way, Oran. And the waters get too hot down south. Once you're beyond the Green Sea you're into the Boiling Straits, and the heat will warp your boat. If you're not already unconscious from the humidity.'

Just as she had with the whalebone cithara, Oran found the story as tantalizing as it was terrifying. There was just so much of the world she didn't know about. So much of the world that *no one* knew about.

The land reared up as the sun sank, and Oran could see the crags of the sea cliffs and a shiver of dark pine forest. The shore was dotted with tall, conical rocks, ribbed red and mauve and deep yellow.

'Aha,' said the captain. 'Looks like we'll beat them to it.'

'Beat who?'

'The whelks.'

She pointed at the rocks. Oran watched. At first she thought it was a trick of the shadows, but the longer she looked, the clearer it became. The rocks were moving. They swayed from side to side and the water foamed around their bases, leaving a broad bow-wave behind them.

'They can't be—' said Oran. 'My da eats whelks on toast!'

'Sea snails get a bit bigger in the open sea,' said the captain.

The *Overture* came up almost alongside them, and Oran could see, in the dying light, a thousand more iridescent colours in the coil of the whelks' shells. They were as tall as the ship's mainmast. When the whelks became aware they had company, they raised their grey, muscular horns from the water and watched the Opera sailing by. They didn't seem concerned. They had no need to be, Oran thought. A blow from their appendages would have broken the ship in half; a collision with one of their colossal shells would have dashed the hull to splinters.

Once the sea snails were behind them, a cluster of lights was visible to the south, along with a magnificent lighthouse three or four times the size of the one on Little Drum. Alick disappeared from the crow's nest and reappeared at her side.

'Harbour's there. Stonefirth, I'm guessing.'

'That's right,' the captain said. 'We're heading straight for the Jaws.'

'The Jaws?' said Alick, with trepidation.

'Don't be put off by the name. It's just the estuary. There's a reason the Headland is called what it's called. Looks like a face, pointing westwards. That promontory there' – she pointed to the lighthouse, which was growing to a size Oran didn't think possible – 'is the Nose, and the one that you can't see in the mist is the Chin. We need to strike a course between them. Into the Jaws.'

'I thought you said we didn't want to be seen?' said Oran.

'We'll change our clothes and our sails, tell them we're merchants. I've got it all figured out, my girl, don't you worry.'

Oran held the wheel steady. The crew took down their pennants and exchanged their purple and gold sails for plain white canvas. Then they changed into clothes that were, somehow, even more extravagant than the ones they were already wearing, but which didn't show off the Opera's famous skein.

The sun dipped into the ocean behind them. Cold seeped into Oran's bones. The plan to break into the Court, to steal from the Duchess, had suddenly gone beyond the realm of a mere idea. It was real, now – real like the Headland itself, vast, complex, impossible to know or see in its entirety.

The *Overture* came into port just as the stars came out. They put down the gangplank and half a dozen members of the Opera trooped out on to the quayside. Too many of them would have been suspicious, it was decided. Oran stayed close to Guillam. When he stepped on to dry land he stopped and raised a finger.

'Listen to that,' he said.

'What?' said Oran. 'I can't hear anything.'

He raised his eyebrows. '*Exactly.*'

They decided to spend the night in a seafront tavern, six of them plus Alick. Oran kept the pouch of his ashes against her hip. It felt good to have him close by. As well as Oran, Alick, Guillam and the captain there were three others: Sev, the quartermaster who had made fun of Oran when she was scrubbing the deck; Erikah, the young woman who had been lookout before Alick; and a man called Korro, one of the gunners.

The tavern was a strange place. In fact, Oran wouldn't have even called it a tavern, since it lacked most of the things that would have defined a place as such. When they came through the front door the quiet was unnerving. There was no music, obviously, but the conversations also seemed dull and unenthused. No ghosts, either, and their lack made an already damp and gloomy establishment damper and gloomier still. The patrons chewed on their mugs of ale, as though it was a chore to be drinking there at all.

She didn't know how many people had spotted Alick hovering beside her, but a ripple of surprise passed through the tavern and he disappeared instantly. The barman watched the group as they made for a table in the rear, scowling as he forced a dirty dishrag into a tankard.

'Kelp juice all round, is it?' said Guillam as the others drew up stools in the cubbyhole.

Oran groaned without meaning to.

'Not a fan, Oran?' said Guillam in mock surprise. 'Captain, remember that stuff we got given on Eyelet? They'd distilled it from cuttlefish. You'd think it would be foul, but you know when something comes full circle, passes all the way through foul and somehow becomes delicious again? Well, this cuttlefish brew was something like that. But mark my words, it put hairs on your chest. Or the opposite. Made your hair fall out. Sev, you drank rather a lot of it, didn't you?'

Sev had a bald head, and an extensive collection of scars, and looked quite the most hardened brute on the Four Seas. But he also smiled a lot and his voice had an unexpectedly musical lilt to it.

'Guillam?' he said.

'Yes?'

'Stop talking and get the drinks.'

'Ah, touched a nerve?'

'*Guillam!*' snapped the captain.

'Yes, yes. So, Oran, what will it be after all that?'

Her tongue was dry, her lips tattered and salty. 'Don't any of you ever drink water?'

'Difficult to come by fresh stuff, most of the time.'

Guillam shrugged. 'But I'll see what I can rustle up for you.'

While he was gone, the rest of the Opera talked in low voices. So low, in fact, it was difficult to hear exactly what they were saying.

'Lot of money here tonight,' said Erikah, looking around at the finely dressed patrons. She tugged down her sleeves and pulled up her collar to conceal her tattoos.

The captain nodded. 'All here for the Hunters' Ball,' she said.

'Hunters' Ball?' said Oran.

'Hosted by the Duchess every year. All the wealthiest merchants get an invite. And, for one year only, the six of us.' She patted a leather satchel that she'd brought with her from the ship. 'There's a forger in the Green Sea who really knows his stuff.'

'The Hunters' Ball?' said Oran. 'How do you have a ball without music?'

'Well, quite,' said Sev. 'It used to be a riot, when I was a child. You could hear it on both sides of the Jaws. That was a lot of years ago. Now it's a horrendously boring affair, but the name has stuck.'

'You grew up here?'

'Sev's the only one of us who's actually from the Headland,' said the captain.

'So, we have invitations to the party,' said Oran.

'Then what?'

'Then your friend – wherever he is – goes snooping for the museum. Shouldn't take long, thanks to your lovely map. He can find the best route, spot any guards we might need to avoid. When he finds the collection, we leave our hosts. Erikah here's the best lockpicker on the Four Seas.' Erikah made a mock bow. 'Sev and Guillam can talk us out of any trouble, and if it comes to a fight we've got me and good old Korro.'

She slapped Korro on the shoulder and it made a dull sound, like meat hitting the butcher's slab. Korro had a complexion to match, so red-faced he was almost purple, veins throbbing at his temples. He was all muscle. He just nodded and smiled.

'Are we just going to walk out of there with all the instruments?'

'No, no! It's much more cunning than that. The Court's latrines hang over the edge of the firth and drop into the river. The others on the ship will bring a boat round and we'll lower the instruments down one by one. Then it's back to the *Overture*, we'll say our farewells and be away before dawn.'

'What do you mean our farewells?'

'You're not coming with us, are you? I thought you were going to confront the Duchess yourself.'

'Oh yes,' Oran said vaguely. 'I forgot.'

The thought of it still troubled her, even now the whalebone cithara was within her grasp. She wanted to play it and had long since given up trying to convince herself otherwise. And it seemed ridiculous to come all this way and then not sing for the Duchess, as she'd always planned to from the moment she'd left the Broken Bottle. But what would she even play? And what about Bard's warning?

'So,' said Erikah, lighting up her clamshell pipe, 'how are you planning on doing it?'

'Doing what?' said Oran.

'Getting an audience with the Duchess.'

Oran didn't know. She hadn't thought of the practicalities of it. 'I could play for her at the Ball,' she said, in a moment of inspiration she hadn't properly thought through.

'Very bold,' said Erikah. 'You'd be playing for the whole Court. All the lords and ladies. Very exposed. Very dangerous.'

'But I'd have the whalebone cithara,' said Oran, trying to convince herself as much as the others.

'You might not even need it,' said the captain. 'You stopped a storm and beat the Greymers with some twopenny guitar. Charming the Duchess will be a piece of cake. The biggest problem will be getting in front of her with *any* kind of instrument.'

That gave Oran a lot to think about.

While she ruminated, Guillam finally returned from the bar with a tray of drinks. They all came in identical wooden tankards. He was humming happily to himself, pleased with his haul. The captain's eyes widened. The rest of them looked at their laps.

Guillam broke into song.

I won't take a husband, I won't take a wife,
A bottle of whisky's my partner for life!

He looked around the table. The crew grimaced and hid their faces.

'Sea's teeth, did somebody die while I was away?'

A silence had expanded to fill the whole tavern, and the patrons were staring at the Opera. Their expressions were a curious mixture, Oran thought, of surprise, fear, sadness, hopefulness. It was as though they wanted Guillam to continue his ditty, and were desperate for him to stop, at exactly the same time.

The barman shouted over their heads, 'No! *No!* You stop that right now! I'm trying to run a business here, and you're going to get me shut down!

Guillam clapped a hand over his mouth.

'You can stay somewhere else tonight,' said the barman. 'All of you. And just be thankful I don't go telling the Duchess!'

⇒17⇐

After a little negotiation and a lot of bribery, the captain persuaded the landlord to let them stay, minus Guillam. He went back to the ship, scolded.

Oran got a tiny room to herself, whose only furnishings were a nightstand, a blubber lamp and a chamber pot. She placed Alick's ashes on the nightstand and got into the bed. She was exhausted. Alick appeared again, his light the colour of butter, as though morning had arrived earlier than it should have. He stared out of the window.

'I can't get used to the silence,' he said. 'It's like a headache.'

'I know what you mean,' said Oran, drawing the blanket up around her chin. 'Just hearing a few lines of that song from Guillam, it was like . . . coming up for air.'

'I hate being the only ghast here too.'

'Is this what Little Drum will be like? If the Duchess gets her way?'

'I suppose so.'

They were quiet for a moment. Oran desperately wanted to sing, or hum, or whistle, but thought she couldn't risk being heard by one of the other patrons. So she just stared at the ceiling and sang in her head.

She realized that this was the longest she'd ever been away from the island. She'd never been absent from her family for more than two nights in her whole life. And she suddenly understood, in this cold and quiet and unfamiliar bed, why that was the case.

'I miss home,' she said.

'So do I,' said Alick.

'What do you think they're doing right now?'

'I think your maw is storming around the island looking for you. I think your granny has organized a secret orchestra in the woods. And I think your da is making more pies than anyone knows what to do with.'

Oran rolled over in her bed and smiled. She liked that idea. Even the bit about Maw. But she couldn't help thinking of a very different scene: her family, sitting at home in silence, wrought and tired with worry. That, she thought, was rather more likely.

'Do you think we've done the right thing?'

'I suppose,' he said.

'You don't sound too sure of yourself.'

'The other ghasts said . . .' He trailed off.

'What? What did the ghasts say? When?'

'Nothing.'

'Don't hide things from me, Alick.'

He fell silent.

'It's about the cithara, isn't it? You know something about it, don't you?'

'I know enough to know that I don't want you to play it.'

'Why not?'

'It's too dangerous. You know the stories. You know how dangerous it is in the hands of the wrong player.'

'But I might be the *right* player.'

'Oran, you need to start listening properly.'

'Says the boy with one ear.'

He gave her a grim look. 'That wasn't funny,' he said.

'You didn't hear the Greymers,' she said. 'They said I played the Old Music. They *bowed* before me, Alick.'

'And now you've got a taste for it?'

'What's that supposed to mean?'

'Isn't that why you're looking for the whalebone cithara in the first place? You don't just want the Duchess to bow to you, or the Greymers. You want *everyone* to think you're the best cithara player on the Four Seas.'

'Well, if you'd actually heard me playing, perhaps you'd think so too.'

Alick took on a flame-coloured tinge. 'In case you needed reminding,' he said, 'the reason I didn't hear you play was because you *abandoned* me in the hold of the ship.'

'I didn't abandon you!'

'I came with you, Oran, because I thought you wanted to help the island. If I'd known this was all just to satisfy your ego, I wouldn't have bothered.'

'Ach, you sound just like Maw!'

'Good. Your maw is wiser than you.'

'I can't believe I'm hearing this.'

'The captain's wiser than you too. But you don't listen to her, either.'

'Yes I do!'

'You listen to her when she's telling you how brilliant you are. But you miss everything else. "The soloist is only as good as the musicians who accompany her", Oran. Does that ring a bell?'

'Of course it does!'

'Then take it to heart. You need to make up your mind whether you're doing this because you want to save Little Drum, or because you want to be the star of the show. I don't think you can have both.'

Oran huffed and rolled over in her bed. It wasn't fair. She'd never asked for her talent. It was starting to feel like the thing that she loved most in the world, the thing that made her most herself, was also some terrible burden she was forced to carry. She was the best player on the island. Maybe on the Four Seas. It was all anyone ever told her. But now she had started admitting it herself, she was accused of being selfish and superior. So what was the answer?

She stared at the wall, waiting for Alick to say something else. 'Sorry', for starters. It never came. His light went out, and she fell into troubled sleep.

The Opera were no lovers of early mornings, and the following day was no exception. Oran was awake for at least two hours before she heard stirring in the room next to hers. The captain and the others emerged from their beds looking like they'd slept in all their finery, and they went down to the tavern's common room. The landlord grudgingly served them breakfast, especially grudgingly since Korro ate as much as the rest of the Opera put together.

Oran stepped out with the pouch of Alick's ashes hanging on her belt, and while she knew he was close, he didn't show his face.

In the daylight she was finally able to see Stonefirth properly. The estuary was more of an archipelago. The mouth of the river was so wide the opposite side was nearly lost in mist, and the water was cluttered with islands of red sandstone. The city covered both riverbanks and all of the islands – it looked, Oran thought, as though it had washed up there – and every part was connected in a web of huge bridges.

On the largest island – a great, rust-coloured mushroom – stood the Court. It looked like a sandcastle left out in the rain. Sandstone was much softer than the granite of the Far Isles, and the Court was older than any building on Little Drum. The turrets and battlements were in the slow process of being scoured away by the weather.

'A wreck, isn't it?' said Sev.

'It isn't what I expected.'

'We've got bets on what's going to be washed away first – the Court, or the island itself.'

Oran was surprised by how pretty the rest of the city was. Streets of narrow, neat, sandstone houses wound around each other like an intricate, layered puzzle. Stonefirth seemed to have at least three 'storeys', and the network of bridges continued within the islands as well as between them. Pretty, thought Oran, but dead. No music, no ghosts. A beautiful husk of a city.

The Opera spent the day buying even more adornments. Oran went with Guillam through the warren of the city buying rings and brooches and jewel-encrusted monocles – all the things that would make them look as though they belonged at the Hunters' Ball. Guillam got himself a pair of heels that rivalled Lord Magmalley's, so high they were practically stilts. He got his face powdered and his nails coloured and had a man artfully apply a mole to his cheek with a paintbrush. Oran looked around for Alick, hoping for a good laugh, but he still seemed to be sulking and wouldn't speak to her.

The last thing to do was to find an outfit for Oran that would suggest she was a rich merchant's apprentice. She spent hours in the silence of a tailor's shop, trying on blouses and pantaloons of whisper-soft silk. She thought that being rich suited her rather well. The tailor said as much, complimenting her on her willowy frame, and she imagined her maw snorting in derision. Guillam added the finishing touch by lending her one of his false moustaches, so the Duchess wouldn't recognize her. It turned out that none of his facial hair was, in fact, real, and he kept a range of different coloured beards and moustaches in a pocket of his waistcoat.

Late in the afternoon they all convened in another
gloomy, tuneless alehouse. The captain had chosen it
specifically as somewhere they could huddle in the
darkness and discuss the evening's strategy. Oran sat
with her cup of untouched kelp juice while the crew
went over the details. Her mind was elsewhere.

'Oran?' Guillam's grinning face was suddenly in
front of hers.

'Sorry. I was miles away. What did you say?'

'Is he here?'

'Who?'

'Your ghast.'

She felt a little itch of displeasure at that. 'He's not
mine,' she said. 'And he's got a name.'

'Yes, of course. Sorry. Alan. Is he here? We need to
talk tactics.'

'He's called *Alick*, And he's here. He's just in a bad
mood.'

She patted her hip, and her blood ran cold. The
pouch of Alick's ashes wasn't there. She'd untied it
while in the tailor's shop. She must have left him
behind!

Oran leapt up, knocking her chair backwards, and
ran out of the alehouse. She was aware of Guillam
half-heartedly following her, before his wheezing
disappeared into the crowds. She sprinted back to the

tailor's, only half remembering the way and losing herself twice in the labyrinth of alleys and bridges and staircases. The problem was that the city existed on several planes. Sometimes she would arrive at the place where she thought the shop had been, only to find that she was directly below it, or above it.

When she finally arrived, sweat-drenched under her silks and velvets, the place was closed. She hammered on the door but no one answered, and the passers-by began to give her strange looks. She looked through the window but couldn't see the bag anywhere. She tried around the back, asked the neighbouring silversmith, who was just shutting up shop. He had no idea what she was talking about. At last she resorted to running through the streets, shouting Alick's name in all directions, but he didn't reply.

The truth that she didn't want to face was this: it wasn't just that he was refusing to talk to her. Something else was missing. There was always a feeling she had when Alick was nearby, a tingle on the back of her neck, but she felt nothing. She closed her eyes and listened hard. Silence. It was like he wasn't even on the Headland, let alone in the city.

Tired and alone she made her way back to the alehouse. The Opera were loitering outside, looking agitated.

'Where've you *been*, lassie?' said the captain. 'The ball starts in an hour!'

'He's gone,' she said, barely able to hold back the tears. 'I left him in the tailor's place, and now he's gone.'

'Who?'

'Alick!'

'Hush, now,' said the captain, looking around at her crew. 'Let's not draw attention to ourselves.' The alehouse had filled up as the day had gone on, and the patrons were spilling into the street.

'What do we do now?' said Oran.

'Well, we'll just have to go ahead without him.'

'I don't mean about the *plan* – I mean, what do we do about *finding* him?'

'Oh, he'll turn up,' said the captain cheerily.

'What if he doesn't? What if he's been stolen? Or thrown out?' She listened for him again. 'I don't even think he's anywhere in the city!'

'I know you're upset, Oran,' said the captain, 'but we'll have to deal with this later. The Hunters' Ball starts now, with or without us. This is the only chance we'll get to find our way into the Court. If you want to find your cithara, or sing for the Duchess, or both, we have to leave. We've still got your map. You haven't lost that, have you?'

Oran felt inside her velvet jacket. Bard's tattered

piece of sea lettuce was still there. Yes, she'd remembered that, and forgotten about her best friend.

'It's here,' she said.

'Jolly good. In that case, you might need to be the one who goes looking for the museum. We'll mingle with the Duchess in the ballroom and keep her busy. Once the fireworks start, that's our cue to start unloading the instruments.'

Oran stared miserably at the sketch of the Court. What was she supposed to do? Everyone on Little Drum was counting on her, though they didn't know it. She could hardly give up on what she had come for.

'Oran?' said the captain. 'Can you do that for us?'

She nodded.

'That's the spirit.'

The six of them set off for the court, all of them laughing and joking apart from Oran.

Guillam was the only one who noticed. He clapped her on the back and said: 'Don't worry, I'm sure you'll find Alan when this is all over.'

Oran didn't bother to correct him. She walked on in her heavy finery, looking for Alick's face in every shadow, listening for him in every patch of silence.

⋟18⋞

The evening sun was the same colour as the stones when the six of them approached the Court. They made their way across the great bridge that joined the north bank of Stonefirth to the Court. The waters of the estuary were a green stew of river and seawater. The bridge was lined with guards in the blood-red skein of the Duchess.

Oran would have been more fearful, were it not for the sight of the other lords and ladies attending the Hunters' Ball. Even the captain looked demure by comparison. The men seemed to be locked in a serious, unspoken competition to see who could wear the tallest hat and widest trousers. The women's fish-bone corsets were so tight they could barely move, their chins sinking slowly into their chests from the weight of their beehive hairstyles. Lords and ladies alike wore exquisite skeins, so long they dragged on the floor or tangled around their feet.

They threw disdainful glances at the Opera's company.

'Well, this won't do,' muttered the captain. 'I'm *always* the best-dressed in the room.'

'Unless I'm in it,' said Guillam.

Erikah sighed. 'We're not having this argument again,' she said.

They arrived at the portcullis of the Court, and the captain produced their forged invitations for the foot-men. The Opera were far better at inhabiting their roles and seemed to forget that Oran was not an actor. She adjusted her moustache and puffed out her chest. She thought this might make her look more self-important, but it also made her heart rattle more hollowly beneath her ribs. She wished Alick was there. She hadn't appreciated just how much he reassured her, even when he was worrying about something.

She stopped. The footman looked at her. One side of the moustache was lower than the other, she could feel it. He frowned, and waved her in.

The Court was as much like a sandcastle inside as it was outside. It was a gloomy, briny place that seemed to leak salt water from the brickwork. The Hunters' 'Ball', as far as Oran could see, consisted of talking very loudly and eating every kind of seafood under the sun. It was a landscape of edible creatures, dead and alive: pyramids of stacked crabs, platters of tunnies, snappers and gurnards, tiers of multi-coloured roe, spitted hunks of whale meat, crispy wispfish scratchings. In the corner nearest the entrance, servants were carving slices from an oyster the size of Oran's old boat.

The Opera party passed the whole length of the hall, nodding and bowing, shaking hands, kissing hands, complimenting anyone and everyone on some absurd detail of their formalwear. They dispersed through the crowd without Oran realizing what they were really doing. Alick was right. They *were* professional thieves.

Soon she and the captain were alone. They paused briefly next to a spinning table of fish eggs, arranged in spokes of black, pink and yellow. It was quieter here.

'Right,' said the captain, 'time for you to do your thing.'

'My thing?'

'Best idea would be to find a way out through the

kitchens. Don't let anyone stop you. Remember, you're a *Magshaw* tonight, and one of the wealthiest merchant families in the Four Seas. Act like you're better than everyone, and people will tend to agree with you.'

Something about that reminded Oran of her argument with Alick, which only made her more nervous.

'Stop that,' said the captain suddenly.

Oran froze. 'Stop what?'

'You're drumming with your fingers.'

'Am I?'

She looked at her hand, resting on the edge of the table. She hadn't realized.

'I do it when I'm nervous too,' said the captain with a small smile. 'But we can't afford to draw any attention while we're here. Humming, whistling, clicking. It all counts as music far as the Duchess is concerned. She is truly out of her *mind*.'

A slice of shadow came between them.

'Your first time at the Hunters' Ball, is it?'

The captain kept her cool admirably. She was no doubt used to being discovered in places she wasn't meant to be. Oran was not so practised. She audibly gasped. It was the Duchess.

'Your Grace!' said the captain. Her accent changed instantly. She bowed low and spread her arms as

though she was trying to ▨▨▨
is quite the most astonishing feast ▨▨
pleasure of attending. Your generosity ▨▨
measure.'

The Duchess waited for the captain to rise. 'Well?'
she said.

'Your Grace?'

'You haven't answered my question. Is it your first
time at the Hunters' Ball?' ▸

The Duchess was still in the dour, funereal dress
she'd worn when she'd visited the Broken Bottle. Her
make-up was as thick as one of the Opera's theatrical
masks. Again, Oran was struck by how little she
matched up to her description in the song. She was
tall and imperious but there was also something
fragile about her. Hardly the monster that the captain
had described.

The captain bowed for a second time. 'Ah!
Yes. Indeed it is. We were honoured to receive the
invitation.'

'And who are you?'

'Magshaw, Your Grace. Durran Magshaw from the
Golden Fields.'

'Magshaw? The sweetroot traders?'

'So please Your Grace. A family business.'

'You make it sound so quaint. Last I heard, the
Magshaw dynasty owned more land than I did.'

The Duchess made no expression – or perhaps she did, but her white, waxy make-up concealed it. That low voice Oran remembered well, almost a man's voice. A difficult pitch. Oran could well believe that she couldn't sing.

'Aha. An exaggeration, I'm sure,' said the captain.

'And this?' The Duchess nodded at Oran. Oran's eyes darted away.

'A nephew of mine. Taking his apprenticeship with the company. A very gifted merchant, I should add.'

The Duchess came forward. It was rare for Oran to be in the company of somebody taller than her. Her mouth was dry, and the smell of warm fish eggs coming from the table was nauseating. To make matters worse, a small crowd of lords and ladies had formed around them, no doubt annoyed that these two unknowns should be getting all of the Duchess's attention.

'He has fingers like my sister's,' the Duchess said, taking Oran's hand in hers. 'A musician's fingers.'

She fairly spat the word. Oran froze. Her throat constricted to nothing.

'I can assure you, Your Grace,' said the captain, 'she has never so much as looked at an instrument.'

'She?'

'He. I mean *he*. Listen to me! Too much of your delicious wine already. You must tell me the vintage, incidentally . . .'

Oran twitched her false moustache. The Duchess let go of her hand, stared at her, then turned back to the captain.

'Why aren't you wearing your signet ring?' she said.

Then came the first crack in the captain's character. The tiniest fraction of a pause. 'We are having them re-foiled,' she said. 'The irritating thing is, we wanted them finished in time for the ball, but the sluggards didn't get the job done in time. Needless to say that particular jeweller won't be receiving the patronage of the Magshaw family any time soon! Ha!'

'I mean the signet rings I sent with the invitations. It is tradition.'

'Ah. Yes. Well. They seemed far too precious to wear in public. They went straight into the family vault.'

Oran could feel the trap closing around them. She looked around at the gathered lords and ladies, who themselves seemed to have scented blood. None of them were wearing signet rings either.

'Remind me,' said the Duchess, 'which design did I give the Magshaws?'

'Design? Well, blow me down, I'm not sure I studied the thing close enough . . .'

The Duchess laughed. 'Please, be at ease, Madam Magshaw,' she said. 'I am only playing with you.'

The captain sagged a little with relief. It was a dead giveaway.

'I sent no rings with the invitations,' the Duchess added.

The captain gaped like a speared fish. She made a noise as though she was trying to laugh along with the others, as though she was part of the joke. But there was to be no escape.

'So the rings in your family vault,' the Duchess pressed. 'Which rings are those?'

'I, er, well, you see, Your Grace——'

'Yes, I see.' She smiled again, and the make-up around the corners of her mouth cracked like the top of a meringue. She spoke over her shoulder. 'Seize them.'

The captain sprang backwards and hurled the tiered table of fish eggs in front of them. The lords and ladies, eager to capture the Duchess's prey, went slithering over the floor, covered in the pink, oily delicacy.

'Time to go, Oran,' shouted the captain, jumping up on to one of the long banqueting tables. She dashed down the length of the hall, kicking mussels and shrimp and cauldrons of chowder over her pursuers. The other members of the Opera had also realized things had gone awry. Korro had a guard in each hand and proceeded to clash them together like a pair of cymbals. Erikah leapt and danced among the grasping hands with the ease of salmon swimming downstream. Sev and Guillam were nowhere to be seen. They had hidden themselves, or already left.

Oran didn't have the strength or the speed or the experience of eluding guards that the others had. She watched the captain's beautifully sequinned robe disappear into the chaos while a pair of Court guards seized her by the shoulders.

The situation was so hopeless she didn't even struggle against the guards' hands. She nursed a silent anger at being abandoned by the Opera. Alick had been right, as usual. Why should she have expected anything more from a gang of pirates?

⇒19⇐

Oran was led out of the ballroom in handcuffs. From there she was taken to a courtyard, purpling in the last of the sun, and down into a square pit in the ground. She could just hear the commotion of the Opera's escape over the battlements.

The Court's dungeons were as deep as the palace was high. At what felt like a hundred fathoms under the earth they came to a labyrinth of tunnelled sandstone and rusted iron bars. Her gaolers threw her in the first cell they came to and left without a word, taking the only light with them. Oran tore off her false moustache for good and threw it into the darkness. She could hardly see her hand in front of her face. The sound of the other prisoners came to her as quiet scuffles and low murmurs. Or was that rats? Or worse? The cells dripped incessantly.

She was more alone than she had ever thought it possible to be. No family, no Alick, no instrument. She missed her cithara more than ever. Since she was born she'd slept with it in her bed every night, and since she'd been old enough to play it there hadn't been a day when the two of them hadn't made music together. The Opera's guitar had been a poor substitute, but at least she'd had something beneath her fingers. Now they twitched in the pitch black. They already felt weak and unwieldy.

And where was Alick now? She tried to tell herself he was somewhere safe, but it wasn't hard to imagine what the tailor would have done with an old bag full of dust. She sang his hearth song, but without an instrument and without his voice to accompany her, it was a cold and lonely lay.

She sang into the darkness, not caring who heard her. The prison seemed to lighten, and for a moment her heart leapt. It wasn't Alick. The brightness was coming from outside her cell, yellow and waxy and not at all like ghast-light. Whoever brought the light had a body of flesh and blood.

Oran shut her mouth, and the song continued for a few bars without her. Then silence. Footsteps. The light grew brighter still. Someone was coming to punish her for singing, no doubt. The guards. The Duchess herself, perhaps.

A blubber lamp appeared from around the corner. It was followed by a skinny arm, then by a skinny boy, dressed in a long nightshirt and a ridiculous pointed nightcap that flopped over one ear. His skin was so pale it had a blue tinge to it. He could have been a ghost — a poor imitation of Alick. His nose was running uncontrollably. His upper lip glistened in the lamplight.

'Don't stop,' he said. His voice was as watery as his complexion.

Oran just looked at him.

'You're very young for a pirate,' said the boy, wiping his nose on his sleeve.

'I'm not a pirate,' said Oran.

'The Duchess says you are.'

'The others were pirates,' she said. 'I'm not one of them. They picked me up when my boat sank.'

'Oh,' said the boy. He sounded disappointed. 'I would have liked to meet a pirate. I watched the rest of your crew escaping from the window. I know exactly where they're hiding. Of course, no one will think to ask me. They'll think I'm just trying to get attention.'

He gave another long sniff. He was very sickly, Oran thought. What on earth was he doing down in the dungeons? Perhaps he was a servant? An errand boy? At any rate he didn't seem much of a threat; but neither did it seem he would be much help.

'Who are you?' she asked.

'I'm Dugald,' he said.

There was a period of silence. He didn't elaborate.

'What are you doing down here?'

'I went to the kitchens to get some milk and sweetroot. On the way back I heard your song.'

'I wasn't singing.'

'Don't lie. I've got good ears.'

Oran held her tongue.

'Where are you from?' the boy asked. 'Can I guess?'

'If you want,' she said slowly.

She didn't know what to make of him. She didn't feel like the boy wished her any ill, but after what had happened at the Hunters' Ball she was wary of walking into another trap.

'Somewhere in the Far Isles, I think,' the boy said. 'You haven't got the accent of any of the Fingers. I think you're from Great Drum or Little Drum.'

She was impressed, and it obviously showed on her face. He gave a shy smile.

'I thought so,' he said. 'My family came from Little Drum, a long time ago. My great grandmaw, I think.

My maw's always been embarrassed about it, but my aunt used to tell me all about your island. About the ghasts. You have birth instruments, don't you? I think it sounds wonderful, to have a companion like that, from the day you're born.' He came forward and peered through the bars. 'You look like a cithara player to me. Yes. You have the hands for it.'

'How do you know that?'

'I'm a cithara player too.'

'How can you be? Music isn't allowed here.'

'It wasn't always this way. I used to get lessons from my aunt. Before she died.' He looked glum – so much like Alick! – and then suddenly brightened. 'I could get you a cithara if you want!'

'How? Where? I thought the Duchess had confiscated all of them.'

'She has,' said the boy, 'but I know where to find them. I could get you a new instrument, and I could get you out of here. Then you could be my new teacher! You could take me back to Little Drum with you!'

Oran got up and came to the front of the cell, twining her long fingers around the cold iron bars. She looked the boy over. He was about the same age as her. He was as slim as her too, and had the very dark hair of the Far Islanders. But there was something else, that indescribable feeling of sameness when meeting someone who shared her birth instrument. He wasn't lying. She could spot another cithara player a mile away.

'Who are you?' she said. 'Really?'

'Why does it matter?' he said. The boy looked affronted, as though he might burst into tears.

'I need to know you aren't trying to trick me,' she said. 'My maw's always telling me I'm too gullible, and I'm in enough trouble as it is.'

He brushed his nightcap out of his eyes and opened his mouth but stopped short of answering. There were more footsteps, heavier than the boy's. Firelight washed around the corner of the passage, followed by a pair of guards. Oran retreated into the darkness. The boy turned and froze.

One of the guards took another step forward. He glanced at Oran, then at the boy.

'Your Grace,' he said. 'The Duchess has asked that you return to bed.'

'I don't want to go to bed,' said the boy. 'I'm not tired.'

'You really shouldn't be down here.'

'Who are *you* to tell *me* where I should and shouldn't be in my own home! You tell my maw— Tell her— Tell her—'

The boy sneezed violently, spraying the guard's face. The man bowed and surreptitiously wiped his cheek with a gloved hand.

Oran held her breath. She couldn't believe what she was hearing.

'Let's get you somewhere warm, Your Grace,' said the guard. 'The cold and the damp aren't good for your condition.'

'I feel fine.'

'Besides, these are dangerous people.' He nodded to Oran. 'You shouldn't be near them.'

'She says she's not a pirate. She says she was shipwrecked, and kidnapped.'

'That's exactly what a pirate would say.'

The boy turned his moist, tremulous face to Oran. His mouth made little, soundless 'o's like a fish. The guard took him by the hand as though he were a child half his age and began leading him away from the cell.

'That's it, Your Grace. Easy does it. How about a story when we get you all tucked in?'

The sound of the boy's sniffing echoed long after they were out of sight. There was the jangle of keys, the thump of a door closing, and Oran was left alone in the pitch black with her thoughts. The outline of the boy and his lantern still throbbed in front of her when she closed her eyes. There was no doubt about who he was. Perhaps things weren't as hopeless as they seemed.

⇒20⇐

Without any windows in her prison, Oran quickly lost track of the time. She slept in darkness, woke in darkness. Her nose, her ears, her hands and her feet were freezing. She practised playing thin air to keep her fingers warm. She listened, as Bard had taught her, for music where there was none: music in the stones, in the iron, in the irregular patter of the rats' feet. Sometimes she thought she heard it. Sometimes she thought she was going mad.

Somewhere in that wasteland of time, the boy appeared again. On this occasion he was holding a lantern in one hand, and a cithara in the other. The light danced off its polished ivory arms.

'See,' he said. 'I told you I could find you one.'

Oran rolled over in the dirt and got to her feet. Her limbs were stiff as new leather. She came forward again and bathed in the lantern's warmth. Dugald was fully dressed this time, in a black velvet jacket and pantaloons with a familiar red skein draped over one shoulder. In amongst the black threads was a curling, silvery snail-trail where he had been wiping his nose.

'You're him, aren't you?' she said. 'You're the Duke.'

He looked at his shiny, buckled shoes, embarrassed. 'So what if I am?'

'*Are* you?'

'I'm the only male Magmorran left. So I suppose I have to be.'

'Magmorran?'

'Family name.'

'So the Duchess is your mother?'

He just shrugged.

It made Oran uncomfortable to think that the Duchess could be related to the people of Little Drum, however distantly. And the fact that she was taking music away from her own son made her seem even more hard-hearted.

'You say your aunt taught you to play?'

'Only a little. My maw didn't like it.'

'And what happened to your aunt?'

He winced. 'Do we have to talk about this? Are you coming with me or not?'

'Coming with you?'

'You can hardly give me a music lesson from inside your cell, can you?' He produced a key from under his skein. 'It's funny what you can get away with when everyone thinks you're too frail to dress yourself.' He sneezed again.

'I don't think this is a good idea,' said Oran, smiling sadly when she heard the echo of Alick.

'Why not? I'm a good student. I said, I've got good ears.'

'I don't mean about the lesson. I mean about your—' She couldn't bring herself to say 'maw'. It sounded so odd. 'About the Duchess.'

'She won't know. She's got to host the Hunters' Luncheon today.'

'You want to go to your chambers?'

'We can take the secret way!' he said, his face lighting up. 'I know all the worm tunnels by heart.'

'Worm tunnels?'

'The lugworms made them, before this was made into a castle. Come! Come!'

He fumbled with the key, opened the door to the cell and took her by the hand. His skin was distinctly slimy in places. Once she was outside, she gently removed her fingers from his.

'It's all right,' she said. 'I can follow you.'

'Fine,' he said, though he seemed disappointed. 'But don't get too far behind, you'll get lost.'

Instead of leading her up the steps the guards had used, he took her deeper into the dungeons. There was a warm and putrid smell of decomposing seaweed.

'It gets fresher as you go up, don't worry,' said the Duke.

'You can't be that frail,' said Oran, covering her nose and mouth against the stink. 'I'd never come through here on my own.'

He turned and beamed.

The cells stopped and the roof became low enough that she needed to stoop. They passed gleaming stalactites and stalagmites, and for a moment Oran could hear the sounds of the sea. They were somewhere at the base of the island. Then they entered another tunnel and began to meander upwards again.

Oran ran her fingers along the wet, ridged walls. 'You said lugworms made these?'

'That's right. A long time ago. Before any dukes or duchesses.'

'Do they still use them?'

'I don't think so.'

Oran tried not to think about what it would be like to come across a worm whose mouth was wider than she was tall.

They burrowed up through the castle until they reached a set of carved steps, which brought them out into an open gallery that ran along one of the walls. Oran was struck with a prickling blast of salt air. Sea and sky were two shades of white. She had no idea what time of day it was.

'Wait a moment,' said the Duke. 'Sometimes there are guards up here.'

He trotted along the arched gallery, looking so slight it seemed the wind would blow him into the sea at any moment. He sneezed twice more, then looked back and beckoned her. They reached one of the Court's sagging towers and passed through a misshapen arch. Inside the Duke produced another key and let them into his bedchamber.

The room was magnificent, or would have been if the curtains had been opened. As it was, everything looked a little dingy in the half-light. On top of the ubiquitous smell of brine was a sweet, floral fragrance – the smell of half-concealed sickness. The centrepiece was a large four-poster bed, draped with puce silk the same colour as the curtains. The bedside table and dresser were piled high with fruit and confectionery and cut flowers, all past their best.

The Duke went and sat on the mattress, then looked at Oran, clutching his cithara.

'How do you want to start, then?' she said.

He struck all the strings with a wayward hand.

Oran winced. 'Well,' she said, coming slowly towards the bed, 'not like that.'

The Duke's face fell, and Oran reminded herself to be patient. She removed some of the debris that had collected on top of the Duke's bedspread — a model boat, a knitted torc, some sweetroot candies in the shape of apples and pears — and sat next to him. She could feel the fever radiating from him, through his velvet jacket. What if he was contagious? Too late now. It was worth getting a fever, anyway, if he knew about the Duchess's collection.

She gently took the cithara from him, as though cradling a baby. She felt a lump in her throat. It wasn't her birth instrument, but even so it felt like embracing a long-lost relative. Its arms were made of ivory inlaid with gold, which she found too flashy, but the strings were old and mellow, unlike the bright sound of her borrowed guitar.

She plucked a chord and felt like she could breathe for the first time in days. She turned to the Duke and smiled.

'First things first,' she said. 'You need to learn how to hold it properly.'

She handed the cithara back to the Duke, rested it on his thigh and manoeuvred his hands into the right position. He squirmed a little when she touched him.

'I can do it by myself . . .' he murmured.

'Hand a little higher.'

'That's not where you put it.'

'If you pluck down there, it'll sound dull.'

'But it's easier.'

'It's a bad habit.'

He huffed.

'That's it. Hand higher. Now relax.'

'I can't relax if I put my hand higher! If I put my hand higher, I have to use my muscles, and if I use my muscles, I can't very well be relaxed, can I?'

Oran took a deep breath. 'If you sit up a little straighter, though . . .'

'I want to learn the song you were singing in the prison! The sad song.'

'That might be a little bit difficult for you,' she said.

The Duke frowned and pursed his lips. His face flushed. 'You don't have to patronize me,' he said. 'We're not all completely talentless on the Headland. My aunt was the best cithara player in the world.'

'I'm sure she was,' said Oran. 'But that doesn't mean she was a good teacher.'

'She was a great teacher!' the Duke protested.

'Why don't you show me something she taught you, then?'

He looked lost. He put his fingers to the strings once or twice but didn't play anything. 'I can't remember any of it,' he said miserably. 'She only gave me a couple of lessons, and then my maw found out, and she stopped me from seeing her. She stopped me even *listening* to her playing. They didn't get on very well, my maw and her sister.'

'I heard,' said Oran.

The Duke shot her a fierce look. 'If you're referring to the rumours, you shouldn't believe everything you hear. My maw might be strange, but she isn't a murderer.'

There was an uncomfortable silence.

'I'm sorry,' said Oran. 'I didn't mean to upset you.'

'She just . . . *changed*. After the shipwreck.'

'The shipwreck?'

'That was how my aunt died. Last year. And my da, and my grandparents. They were all sailing to Harp. Maw had told me I had to stay here, as usual. Didn't want me near Aunt Isla. There was an accident on the way back. They were in a storm and got smashed against the rocks of the Nose. My maw was the only one who survived. And somehow everyone thought she'd arranged the whole thing. Everyone had already made up their minds that they hated her anyway.'

'Why?' Oran asked him. Of course, the song of 'The Red Duchess' made all sorts of wild claims about the Duchess's crimes, but she suspected her son might offer a more honest account.

'I don't know,' he said. 'They just took a dislike to her. I think it was because everyone compared her with her sister. Aunt Isla was so happy all the time. Always smiling, always singing. My maw told me she was mad.' He let out such a big sigh his whole body flopped sideways on to the bed. 'It was all such a mess,' he said.

Oran took his cold hand in hers. She didn't know what to say.

'Is it true,' he said, 'that you can bring back the dead in the Far Isles? With music?'

'We don't bring them back,' she said. 'They never really leave.'

'Oh,' said the Duke. 'I thought, maybe, if I sang the right song, I could see them again. Da, Aunt Isla, Granny and Granda.'

'It doesn't really work like that,' said Oran. 'I'm sorry.'

'Then how does it work?'

'It's difficult to say,' said Oran. 'We have so many songs on Little Drum, going back hundreds of years. Thousands. Everybody learns them. Our whole lives are song. Making music is as easy as breathing, for us.

As important as breathing too. Every song contains a little bit of those who sing it, so when we pass on, the songs keep part of us alive. As a ghost. Does that make sense?'

'Sort of . . .'

'And the ghasts are the ones who *teach* us the songs too. Songs for everything. Songs about the tides, about the seasons, about fishing, about building ships . . . And when we sing them, we keep the Long Silence at bay.'

'So . . .' The Duke frowned. 'The ghasts teach you the songs that keep them alive?'

'That's right. And then, when I take on my ghast-hood, I'll teach my descendants. And so on, and so on. Tradition isn't a line, It's a circle.'

She drew one in the air with her finger. The Duke looked baffled.

'I don't understand.'

'It is difficult to understand, if you haven't grown up with the tradition. That's why your maw doesn't realize how disastrous her new law is.'

Dugald looked at his lap, as if ashamed, and Oran found herself thinking of home again. Talking about it reminded her of what she stood to lose; of what was still to be done.

She put on a smile and turned to the Duke. 'Let's have another go at playing a tune, shall we?'

'But I can't. I just told you.'

'I think we could perhaps try you with a different instrument. It's very important to find one that fits the player.'

The Duke sat up and looked at the gold and ivory cithara. 'I just thought this one looked nice.'

'It is very handsome,' said Oran. 'But it might not be right for you. Are there more in your mother's collection?'

'Lots. They're just upstairs.'

Oran felt a shiver of anticipation. 'And you say the Duchess is occupied?'

'All day.'

'Then could you show me?'

⤜21⤛

The walls and ceiling of the Court made Oran permanently dizzy. There were no straight lines, no right angles. Nothing had any symmetry to it. The whole building was in the process of a slow, thousand-year slump back into the sea.

'We're in luck,' said the Duke as they crept up an uneven spiral staircase in one of the turrets. 'No guards here today. They must have all been sent to look for your pirate friends.'

'They're not my friends,' said Oran unequivocally.

She wondered where they'd got to. The tower had

windows like portholes, giving her a good view over the bay. She couldn't see the *Overture* anywhere, although she wasn't sure she would recognize it with its bright sails furled.

The stairs went no further. They must have been at the highest point of the Court, and the wind whistled through the walls. The Duke stopped outside a warped eelwood door, took out one of his stolen keys and put it in the lock. It clattered around in there as though it was too small, or the lock was too big. He put his shoulder to the wood and pushed, his feet grinding and slipping on the sandstone floor.

Oran pushed with him.

'I can *do* it!' he said sharply. Oran took a step back and left him to struggle. It opened a few inches and then wouldn't budge any further. 'There,' said the Duke. He posted himself through the crack, and Oran followed. She wondered how the Opera would have managed, getting through here. Guillam, in particular.

There was a deep-sea darkness inside the museum. Oran was dimly aware of a great mass of clutter, the way she sensed a reef when sailing at night. There were smells of dust and damp and neglect. The Duke disappeared for a moment and hauled on a rope that hung just inside the door. The drapes opened and the light poured in.

Instruments covered the walls and the ceiling

like fish scales. Hundreds, thousands, so many Oran couldn't see the sandstone underneath. Some were strung up with old fishing nets, others pierced right through their bodies with long iron stakes: citharas, fiddles, guitars, drums, their wood split and stained from the rust. Oran let out an involuntary groan.

'I wish my maw wouldn't do it,' said the Duke. 'Some of them are beyond playing now.'

Even with the curtains open Oran couldn't see how far back the museum went. The Duchess had displayed her finest specimens on the walls and in cabinets, but in amongst these were piles – mountains – of miscellaneous instruments, hidden under dust sheets and waiting to be sorted. There were the instruments of the Chorus – citharas, fiddles, bagpipes – and the instruments of the Opera – guitars, accordions, trumpets, trombones – and many more that Oran had never seen before. There was a huge golden horn, the size of three men lying down. Strange wind instruments in the shape of flatfish, which you played by blowing over their gills. Two ivory boxes, as high as Oran's waist, with pedals at their base and hundreds of strings across their middle. She plucked the lowest of them, and it sent a groan up into the vaulted ceiling.

'This is awful!' said Oran.

'I know.'

'No one ever plays them?'

'No. Most of them are just attracting mildew and sea lice.'

She wound between the pillars but didn't see anything that looked like the instruments Bard had described. But then there were so many. It was, as her granny would have said, like looking for an anchovy in a shoal of sardines.

'Dugald,' she said.

'Yes?' He looked delighted that she'd used his name.

'Have you heard of the whalebone cithara?'

He shook his head. 'No.'

Oran sagged with disappointment. 'Ach.'

'What is it?'

'It's an instrument. A special instrument. Someone told me it would be here.'

'What's so special about it?'

'I don't really know myself. I just know it makes good music. The best music. The kind of music that might change your maw's mind.'

'Change her mind? About what?'

'About everything.'

'And you think I can play it?'

'Well . . .' She thought of Alick, and half wished he was there to disagree with her. But only half. 'Actually,' she said, 'I was thinking of playing it myself.'

'Oh. Well, maybe we can look for it?' He sneezed

and it reverberated through every instrument in the museum. 'What does it look like?'

'I don't know exactly,' said Oran, feeling a little stupid. 'Not very nice-looking. It's made of a whale's jawbone. Very old. Black and sort of twisted and probably covered in barnacles and boneworm.'

'I know the one!' said the Duke.

'You do?'

'Aunt Isla had one just like that.'

Oran frowned. That couldn't be right. What would the Duchess's sister be doing with Bard's instrument?

'I'm not sure we're talking about the same thing,' she said. 'Did you ever hear her play it?'

'A few times,' said the Duke. 'Aunt Isla had loads of citharas, so she didn't play that one very often. But when she did . . .'

He tailed off. Oran was very still. Her body was humming from toes to forehead.

'When she did?'

'It was amazing. It was like the whole world stopped when she played it. Like there was nothing to worry about. Nothing to be afraid of. The song was all there was. I could have listened to her for ever.' He was lost in his thoughts for a moment, then looked up. 'The first time I heard it was the moment I decided I had to be a musician too.'

It all sounded so familiar. How many times had she

felt that way in Bard's company? And that was *without* the instrument.

'Can I see it?' she asked.

Without answering, he shuffled down one of the aisles between the cabinets, left, right, left, into what seemed to be the centre of the museum. The pillars curved inwards and met above their heads like the bulb of a flower. Here, almost untouched by the light from the window, an old canvas sail had been thrown over a collection of objects. He pulled it back, releasing a cloud of dust and mould. He doubled over in a coughing fit.

Underneath was an eelwood chest, some faded red dresses, stacks of paintings in elaborate frames. Dugald went to the chest and began to unfasten the clasps. Oran took one of the dresses in thumb and forefinger, found the silk disintegrated at her touch.

'Here,' called the Duke. He opened the chest and threw the lid back.

Oran thought she could smell the Great Barrow. She came over and stood by him. The whalebone cithara had been wedged inside without any particular care. It hardly looked like an instrument at all. It could have been a piece of driftwood. She ran a hand over its gnarled frame and then withdrew it, suddenly fearful of touching the strings.

'Is this what you meant?' said the Duke.

Oran said nothing. A squall rasped against the tower's windows. She looked down at the cithara, then at the Duke.

'What?' he said. 'What's wrong?'

'How did you say your aunt died?'

'I told you. She was on the ship when it sank with everyone else.'

Another gust of wind shook the tower.

'Dugald,' she said. 'Your aunt is still alive.'

'You can't joke about things like that,' said the Duke.

'I'm serious. I've met her. She's living in the Far Isles. She's my teacher.'

He fixed his eyes on hers. His pupils were wide and dark and quivering. 'Are you sure?'

'She was the one who told me about this cithara.'

There was a dull thud from the museum door. It scraped on the uneven flagstones and she could hear the Court guards curse as they tried to force their way inside.

Oran and the Duke ducked down behind the chest. It was too late to replace the covering, to close the curtains. There was no way they were getting out unseen.

The Duke was still staring at her. 'You swear?' he whispered.

'On the heart of the sea.'

The Duke's face lit up again. 'I could come back with you!'

Oran shook her head. 'Not a good idea.'

'Why not? I could go and live with Aunt Isla. She could teach me too. She could teach both of us.'

'You can't just run away from your family.'

'You did.'

'That was different,' said Oran, but she wasn't sure it was. 'Besides, I don't even know how we'd get home. We'll be lucky to get out of this room.'

The guards finally opened the door. She heard them shuffling into the museum, shifting the instruments, searching under the dust sheets.

'What about your pirate friends?' he whispered.

'They're not my friends, Dugald. And they're long gone.'

'No they're not. I told you. I saw them from my window. Your ship's still here.'

'Really?'

'Really. I can see everything from my bedroom. I watch everyone coming and going.'

Among the sounds of the search they heard the Duchess's voice, directing her men.

'Oh squid,' hissed the Duke. 'My mother's here.'

'Can't you say something to her?'

He shook his head. 'She can't find me with you. We'll both be locked up.'

'Wait!' she hissed. 'Dugald!'

'I'll come back for you. I promise.' The Duke's hand slipped out of hers and he slunk silently away through the debris. He was out of sight in moments.

'Found her!' One of the guards appeared from behind a pillar in a flash of red skein. He lunged.

Oran leapt up and scrambled over the heaps of stolen and abandoned instruments. Another guard planted himself in her way and she ducked left, crashing into a glass cabinet and sending shelves of oyster castanets skittering over the floor. The guards closed in, seized her by the arms and hauled her back to the door, heels dragging in the dust.

The Duchess was waiting for her, still and silent. She was dressed in mourning just as she had been at the Hunters' Ball: a sharp pinnacle of black rock, against which Oran was to be dashed. She couldn't help thinking of all the worst verses of 'The Red Duchess'; all those cruelties, tunefully enumerated.

'I see you've shaved since we last met,' she said in that curiously deep voice. She held up the false moustache that Oran had discarded in her cell, and let it fall to the floor. 'Where is my son?'

'I don't know. Really.'

'You don't know.'

'Don't punish him. It's not his fault.'

'I *know* it's not his fault. Let me guess: you sang him

a song and he promised to do whatever you asked?' The Duchess's face was glacial, her anger cold and weary, and for a brief and confusing moment Oran was reminded of her own mother.

'It's not like that,' she said.

'Can't you see how frail he is?' said the Duchess, and beneath her make-up her cheeks took on a little colour. 'You horrid thing. Taking advantage of him like that. And everyone wonders why I mistrust musicians.'

A pair of guards came back, panting. 'Your Grace,' said one. 'It's gone.'

'What's gone?'

'Your sister's instrument.'

The Duchess swept her eyes over the museum and brought them to bear on Oran – the same burning stare she had used in the Broken Bottle. 'Where is it?'

'I don't know,' said Oran. 'I don't have it.'

'I can see you don't have it. You gave it to him, didn't you? He's going to smuggle it out to your friends, wherever they are.'

Before Oran could reply, the Duchess's eyes widened, and she straightened up.

'She sent you, didn't she?' she said, almost in a whisper.

Oran swallowed. She knew who the Duchess meant.

'She sent you to fetch her cursed instrument for her. Of course! No doubt she thinks she'll return as the great liberator. And everyone will love her for it.' She sounded as if she was almost in tears. 'I knew I was too lenient on her. Why, Tusk is a stone's throw from your island! I'll bet she reeled you in like a fish on a line. Yes, exile was too kind for her. I should have drowned her while I had the chance.'

'Drowned?' said Oran. 'She's your own sister!'

'Exactly! My own sister, and look what she did to me!'

Oran didn't know what she meant by that. The museum was quiet, apart from the nervous shuffling of the guards.

'Perhaps Isla would like me to come for her,' said the Duchess. 'But I won't rise to the bait. I won't come within a hundred leagues of her.' She paused, as though weighing something up. 'But you can send her a message.'

⋙22⋘

It was the most beautiful day Oran had seen since leaving Little Drum. From inside her cell she could see a perfect circle of blue sky, and a breeze blew in the warm, honeyed scent of blossom from the Duchess's garden.

She'd been moved to a different prison. She didn't know why. She'd slept there for one night and it was more comfortable than the one underneath the Court. It had a straw mattress, and the air was drier. No one had visited her, and she'd had nothing but time to think about what had happened. The more she thought about Bard now, the more the woman retreated into the shadows. How much had she not told her? What exactly had transpired between her and the Duchess?

The sunlight fell hot and solid as gold ingots on to the floor of the cell. It couldn't have been far off midday. She stood beneath the little window and let it fall on her face. She thought she could hear waves, distantly, but realized after a moment's listening that the roar wasn't coming from the sea but from the combined chatter of Stonefirth on a busy market day.

There was a shuffle of feet outside her cell. The Duke, perhaps?

The door opened and two guards entered in their red skeins. Their faces were strangely apologetic.

'Time to go,' one of them said.

'Go? Where?'

They didn't reply.

'Is she sending me back home?' Oran asked.

She wouldn't have minded that at all. Though she didn't want to leave without looking for Alick again – the thought of him abandoned in the sludge of the estuary made her sick.

The guards said nothing. They turned and left, leaving the cell door open. Oran followed them out into a courtyard, half in shadow from the castle's largest tower. She had to run to keep up with them.

Their custody of her seemed half-hearted. She tapped one on the shoulder.

'Excuse me? Can't you tell me where we're going? I thought I was meant to be delivering a message?'

He marched on.

'Hello?'

He glanced at her briefly. His great black eyebrows rustled beneath his cloth cap. 'I'm sorry, girl.'

'Sorry? What for?'

Two more guards arrived and together they led her through the huge, sagging mouth of the castle and out on to the same bridge that she had crossed with the Opera two days ago. It was much changed from then. It was deserted, and the stones were white in the heat. The Duchess had stripped Oran of the Opera's rich clothes, and the ground scorched the bare soles of her feet.

The streets on the north bank of the estuary were crowded with people. She heard their low, tidal rumblings more clearly now. As she approached the end of the bridge their voices became hushed. They stared at her. She stared back. The whole town had come out to see Oran, rich and poor, in skeins of a thousand different colours and designs.

The harbour was no different. It was crammed with boats that seemed to have no way of getting in or out. Their crews sat on the bowsprits, the gunwales, the cross beams, shielding their eyes from the high sun. They all watched Oran as she approached. As she left the bridge and stepped on to land, she saw another wooden structure built on the quayside. She realized then what the 'message' was that the Duchess wished to send. The truth of it was so clear and stark and dazzling it left her feeling almost nothing at all.

They were going to hang her.

The walk to the scaffold took hours, days. She stopped once or twice and the guards very gently nudged her onwards again. The numbing inevitability of it all. Ahead of her the circle of rope drifted silently in the wind, waiting for something – some*one* – to weigh it down. Oran played out a hundred different ways of escape, and they all ended with her head in the noose.

The Duchess was sitting in front of the gallows on a slightly raised dais. Dugald was nowhere to be seen. So much for his promise to come back for her.

Oran mounted the scaffold. Her mind presented her with the bizarre but confident theory that she, Oran, was not in fact Oran – that the real Oran was still at home on Little Drum, touring the islands with Alick in her boat, singing songs and catching fish and nibbling the corners of her da's pies. That the Duchess had never even visited the island. That life went on as usual.

She looked at the trapdoor. She looked at the rope.

'We are gathered here today,' rang out the voice of a herald, 'to witness Her Grace's justice meted out upon those who would undermine the state of the Headland and its citizens.'

There was no baying from the crowd. They just listened quietly.

The herald continued. 'Of attempted kidnapping of the royal person of the Duke; of consorting with pirates; of theft and possession of a musical instrument; of conspiring to create a musical song or sound in the presence of Her Grace, in defiance of the Bill of Quietude. Therefore, in accordance with the laws of the Headland and the Duchess, and in light of the severity and manifold nature of her crimes, it has been decided that the accused shall be executed in a manner that befits all criminals of the high seas.'

The hangman began to adjust the noose. He didn't look like he'd done much hanging in his life. He looked more like a baker, or an innkeeper, with a broad, friendly face.

Oran looked out at the crowd. She thought of the other Oran again, the real Oran, back home. She thought of her maw and da, and her granny. She thought of Alick. Thought she could see him, drifting among the onlookers, watching her with his sad, saucer-eyes.

The herald was saying something else now, but she wasn't listening. She squinted against the day, wiped away tears that she hadn't even known were there.

She *could* see Alick. He *was* drifting through the onlookers. He disappeared and reappeared, like a fin cutting among the waves. The others started to see him too. There was a fearful muttering and the crowd began to part. He disappeared.

The hairs on Oran's neck lifted, and she knew he was beside her on the scaffold.

'Don't worry,' he said. 'There's a plan.'

He began to sing in his clear, bell-like treble. Oran's heart swelled. He *never* sang in public.

The captain's a rascal, the bosun's a dog,
The boat's full of holes and we've run out of grog.
We're tired and we're old and we're done with the sea;
But while we can sing we can call ourselves free!

It was an old song. A shanty. The kind of tune that everyone in the Far Isles knew, and that everyone on the Headland should have known. Like so many shanties, the song had a call and a response. Alick sang the first two lines alone, and then, from nowhere, a chorus of voices joined him, ending with that old rallying cry: *But while we can sing we can call ourselves free!*

The Duchess got out of her seat and looked wildly around, thrusting her earplugs into her ears. Oran scanned the crowd. She couldn't see them, but she knew Guillam's voice when she heard it. The captain's too.

Alick kept singing.

The sails are in in tatters, the rudder's askew,
We sailed through the maelstrom and lost half the crew.
We're tired and we're old and we're done with the sea;
But while we can sing we can call ourselves free!

There was a thump of feet now. A beat as strong as her pulse. Oran stamped on the scaffold and it rang like a hollow drum. She sang with him.

My hand's made of iron and my leg's made of wood,
My left eye's a glass eye, my right eye's no good,
We're tired and we're old and we're done with the sea;
But while we can sing we can call ourselves free!

The crowd was joining in now. Their faces were lighting up. The hangman was smiling too, and some of the guards who were feeling brave. Oran heard instruments: trumpets, trombones, accordions. She hadn't felt the pull and push of a song like this since that night in the Broken Bottle. It seized her, bodily. It was like being heaved skyward on the crest of a great wave: the weight of it, and the weightlessness, at one and the same time.

> *I sleep on the gun deck, I long for my bed.*
> *I haven't been watered, I haven't been fed.*
> *We're tired and we're old and we're done with the sea;*
> *But while we can sing we can call ourselves free!*

The Duchess raged around the dais. There were tears in her eyes. 'Stop it!' she screamed. 'All of you! I'll have you hanged along with her!'

They did not stop. Some had even crossed their arms and linked hands, swaying like waves as they roused themselves to mutiny.

> *We're tired and we're old and we're done with the sea;*
> *But while we can sing we can call ourselves free!*

From out of these waves rose the Opera, a dozen of them, hooded and disguised. The captain leapt up on to the scaffold, voice like a bronze gong. Ever the show-woman, she flung her cloak to the floor, shook out her long, braided hair, and bowed to the onlookers. The crowd applauded.

'You came back!' said Oran.

''Course we came back,' she said. 'How were we

meant to sail away without our captain?'

There was a crack of a flintlock pistol. Screams. The song was torn to shreds. The Duchess stood on the cushion of her seat, the barrel pointing to the sky, a cloud of blue-black smoke wafting about her head. She lowered the gun and pointed it at the guards closest to her.

'You have these too, you know,' she shouted. '*Use them.*'

The captain took Oran's hand and hauled her off the gallows. 'This way,' she said, shouldering through the crowd and making for the quayside. 'The *Overture*'s ready to go.'

'I don't understand,' Oran gasped, trying to keep up. 'You found him? You found Alick?'

'He was on the *Overture* the whole time!' said the captain. 'The tailor sent all your old clothes back to the ship with his manservant. Your ghast friend was bundled up in your trousers. Not very happy about it either.'

Oran didn't know whether to laugh or cry. 'Was this his idea?'

'No, no. That was the other lad. He told us you were in trouble.'

'The other one?'

'The snotty one. You make friends quickly, lassie!'

'*Dugald?* How—'

A stray musket ball flew over their heads.

'Now's not the best time for explanations, Oran. Hurry along.'

They leapt from the edge of the quay on to a fishing boat, whose crew watched in astonishment.

'Beg your pardon . . .' said the captain, with a tiny bow.

Strains of the shanty still floated forlornly among the sounds of clashing steel and gunfire. Oran and the captain had to cross the decks of three other ships until they got to the *Overture*, which was moored on the edge of the packed harbour.

The Duke was waiting for her under the mainmast. Alick was there too, a shimmering beside him. She didn't know what to say to either of them. She threw her arms in a wide embrace.

The Duke suddenly cried out: 'Maw! Don't!'

Oran felt it before she heard it, a stinging in the hand she'd been waving with. Her playing hand. She raised her palm in front of her face and examined the wound with a strange calmness. She could see the daylight on the other side of the red hole. Her fingers curled lazily, but when she tried to straighten them they wouldn't move. There was a moment or two of numbness, then a great throb of pain all along her arm, before she fell unconscious on to the deck.

≥23≤

Oran remembered very little of the next few days.
She didn't even know how many days it was.
She lay on the captain's feather bed, drifting in and out
of consciousness. She would dream of playing her
birth instrument, then wake to find her right hand
burning, then force herself back to sleep whether she
was tired or not. Every time she opened her eyes, either
Dugald or Alick was at the foot of the bed. Frequently
she couldn't tell them apart. They were both as pale
and insubstantial and dreamlike as each other.

At some point the fog cleared, and she made the

monumental effort to sit up in bed. Both her friends were in the cabin with her. The Duke was at her bedside with a plate of bread and cheese and a cup of water; Alick was hovering in front of her. She tried to adjust the pillows at her back, forgot about her injury and cried out in pain. The Duke hurried to make her comfortable.

'How is it?' said Alick.

Oran raised her hand and didn't recognize it. It was bound tightly in so many bandages it looked like a stump. There was a faint pink stain in the centre of the fabric that let her know the wound still hadn't healed.

She just shook her head in answer to Alick's question.

'Would you like something to eat?' asked the Duke. He balanced the tray of food on her blankets.

She picked at the bread with her left hand. She felt so weak and clumsy, unable to break it into pieces without two sets of fingers. In the end she tore at it with her teeth like a dog. She washed it down with the water and spoke to Alick first.

'I'm sorry,' she said.

He frowned. How she had missed that furrowed brow! 'Sorry? What for?'

'For leaving you behind.'

'Oh,' he said. 'It's fine.' It plainly wasn't fine.

'It was just an accident.'

'It's all right, Oran,' he said. 'You don't need to make excuses. I know why you did it.'

Oran's heart flushed cold. 'You think . . . you think I did it on purpose?'

'I understand. It must get tiresome having me around. Always complaining. Always worrying. Always telling you not to do things.'

'Alick, honestly, I just forgot.'

'But there's a reason you forgot. Whether you realized it or not, you *wanted* to forget me.'

'That's not true!'

'Seems like you've found a more fitting companion, anyway. Someone as special as you.' He looked at the Duke. 'When we're home, I'll go back to the other ghasts. You won't need to worry about me following you around everywhere.'

'Alick, stop this.'

'What good would I have been when you got caught by the Duchess? Dugald is the one who saved you. And he's the one who stole the whalebone cithara.'

Oran kept looking at him, half sorry, half annoyed by his stubborn self-pity. He nodded to the Duke. She turned in the bed, put too much weight on her hand, winced, and tucked it under her armpit.

'Dugald?' she said. 'You stole it?'

The Duke reached under the bed and drew out a

stained burlap sack. He laid it on the bed next to the tray of food, loosened the drawstring and showed Oran what was inside. There was that distinctive smell of the Great Barrow, a smell of stone and brine and long years.

She peeled back the edges of the sack with her good hand. The whalebone cithara was inside.

'But . . . how?'

'I took it when the guards found us. I just hid in the museum until you'd all left, and then snuck out again.'

'And you told the Opera to come and rescue me?'

He gave one of his bashful smiles. 'It's easy to get out of the Court if you know the worm tunnels. I knew which ship was yours. Some of your friends were lying low in the city, but most were still on board. Including Alick. The song was his idea, by the way.'

'It was a good idea,' said Oran, hoping to reassure her friend. His face was blank and his light was dim and sooty.

She stood the whalebone cithara upright and examined it closely for the first time. It was an ugly thing, twisted and riddled with holes. The strings looked too thick to make music, like seaweed pulled taut. She drew the bag over it, closed it and put it back under the bed with difficulty.

'Well, looks like I was never meant to play it anyway.' She waved her bandaged hand. 'Looks like I'll never play anything again.' She felt the sobs heaping up in her chest, and thrust her hand under the covers so she wouldn't have to look at it.

There was a half-hearted knock at the door followed by a flood of light and gust of cold sea air. The captain stepped heavily into the cabin and folded her arms, her rings and bracelets clinking around her.

'How are you feeling, lassie?' she said.

Guillam peeped into the doorway behind her.

'Miserable,' said Oran.

'Miserable? You're part of an exclusive club now! A good old leftie!'

The captain held up her three-fingered right hand and grinned, but Oran wasn't in the mood for jokes. She looked down at the dry crusts of bread and didn't reply.

'Come now,' said the captain, softening her tone. She sat on the end of the bed and the frame protested under her weight. 'That's how I felt when that blasted clam took half my hand. But you'll play again, just like I did. I had to learn all over again, and it made me twice the player I was before.'

Oran didn't look up. That sounded like nonsense.

'Great,' she said. 'Back to playing "The Laughing Prawn" with all the weans.'

'Aye,' said the captain, 'and don't you knock it.' She lifted Oran's face gently by the chin. She looked deadly serious. 'You'll be surprised how much you find when revisiting the simplest tunes. If you can only play a few notes, you think more about listening than playing. And you'll find the simplest songs contain the most hidden riches.'

It was so rare to see the captain without an extravagant smile. When her face was straight, you really believed her. Perhaps that was what it meant to be a good actor. Even so, Oran thought back to something that Alick had said in their argument: the captain was a good deal wiser than she let on.

'Where are we?' Oran asked, looking through the open door at the sea beyond.

'We've just passed the Spit. We'll have you home before sundown.'

'Home?' said Oran, the word soft and warm on her lips.

'We figured that was the best place for all of us. Get you back to your maw and da, get us as far as possible from the Court. There's a wee complication, though.'

'What's that?'

'We're still being followed. The Duchess's flagship is not more than half a day behind us.'

'I'm not surprised,' said Oran. 'We do have her son,

after all. She must have seen him when she took a shot at me.'

The cabin went very quiet.

'Excuse me,' said the captain. 'Who has whose son?'

'We have the Duchess's son.' She looked at Dugald. His face was the colour of off milk. 'Didn't you tell them?'

The whole ship seemed suspended on the crest of a wave. There was a feeling of held breath in the cabin, and then the *Overture* dipped into a trough and Guillam laughed a loud, incredulous laugh.

'This lad is the *Duke*?' said the captain.

'Didn't any of you know? Alick?'

'Sea's teeth!' cried the captain, getting to her feet. 'As if we weren't the most wanted ship on the Four Seas already! And now we've got the Duchess's son as a hostage!'

'He's not a hostage, he wanted to come.'

'Do you think that makes any difference from the Duchess's point of view?' The captain began to stomp in circles around the cabin. 'We're the Opera, we don't take *hostages*! My old man will be spinning in that squid's belly!'

'I'm sorry,' said the Duke, wringing his hands. 'I didn't want to get anyone into trouble.'

'Well, it's a little late for that, laddie,' said the captain. 'No wonder she's following us. I'll bet she's got the whole of the Headland's navy on our tails. She won't rest until we're all at the bottom of the sea. And don't think she'll stop with us, Oran. I'm sure she'll think of a way to punish Little Drum even further if she thinks your people are harbouring her son's kidnappers.'

The news was spreading through the ship now, and the other members of the Opera were starting to crowd the doorway, muttering and pointing and staring at their fateful stowaway.

Oran's heart and hand began to throb in unison. 'Then we won't go to Little Drum,' she said.

'And where will we go? She's only a day behind us. She'll follow us to the edge of the sea.'

Oran thought for a few moments. She looked at Alick. His eyes were narrowed. 'We stick to the original plan,' she said.

'And what, may I ask, was the original plan?'

'We go to Tusk.'

A fearful murmuring passed through the Opera, who had now almost filled the doorway completely with their faces.

'While I respect you as my fellow captain,' said the captain, 'I cannot agree with that. I know what you're thinking: a barren rock like that will be the last place she'll look for us. And once upon a time that might have been true. But this past year there've been strange tales about Tusk.'

'Aye, those rocks are cursed, and no mistake,' Guillam interjected. 'The best sailors won't go within ten leagues of the place.'

'Why not?'

'It's not empty any more,' said the captain. '*She's* there.'

'She?'

'Aye,' said the captain. 'There's a sea witch who's made her home on Tusk. She'll lure us on to the rocks and do the Duchess's work for her.'

Oran couldn't help smiling at that. 'That witch,' she said, 'is exactly who we're going to see.'

ᗌ24ᗍ

Tusk rose ahead of them like a tree trunk, broken and half submerged. The strains of Bard's sea organ floated out to meet them. The captain had given Oran the wheel but was still standing at her shoulder. She seemed agitated.

'You hear that?' she said.

'Yes,' said Oran. 'That's Bard's sea organ. She carved it into the rocks, so the waves play it.'

'That's how she catches her prey . . .'

Oran laughed, but couldn't help thinking of something the Duchess had said: *I bet she reeled you in like a fish on a line.* In a way that was true — the sound of the organ was the first thing that had led her to Bard. She'd been meaning to sail to the Five Fingers, almost a year ago, but had found herself drawn to the music that seemed to emerge from the sea itself.

'We've been over this,' she said, resting her bandaged hand on one of the wheel's handles. She'd explained to the Opera that Bard was the Duchess's sister, but they'd had a hard time believing her, and were stubbornly superstitious.

'It just seems a fierce strange story,' said the captain. 'The Duchess had all her family killed. Everyone knows that.'

'That's how the song goes. But the Duke says it didn't happen that way.'

'And how did it happen? Because they're definitely dead — you can't dispute that.'

Oran thought. 'I'm not sure. There was a shipwreck. But something else happened. Something between the Duchess and her sister.'

The captain remained sceptical. That was another reason why it seemed a good idea to Oran to go to Tusk. There were still so many questions that needed answering.

The *Overture* sailed within half a league of the island and halted. Oran squinted. There was no one on its grassy top, or on the Bad Steps, or in the mouth of the cave. The whole place seemed deserted. The captain, however, still seemed convinced there was some witchcraft at work.

'If you don't mind,' she said, 'I think we should drop anchor out here. You and the Duke can go ashore in the rowboat, if you like, but you won't get any of the Opera going ashore.'

'If you insist,' said Oran.

'And don't take too long doing whatever you're doing. I don't particularly like the idea of waiting here when the Duchess is only a few hours away.'

'Don't worry about the Duchess,' said Oran. 'Bard will know how to deal with her.'

While the crew prepared the rowboat, she went looking for Dugald and Alick. She found them in the captain's cabin.

'Ready to go?' she said.

Dugald nodded, but he already looked seasick.

'Alick?'

'I'm staying here.'

Oran laughed, but it was very quickly clear that Alick wasn't joking. She had been hoping that the expedition to Tusk would make things easier between the two of them again. The old partnership, back on the high seas. 'Here? On the ship?'

'Yes.'

'Why? Because I'm going to see Bard again?'

'I won't tell you what to do any more. You don't want to listen to me anyway. And that's fine. You can make your own decisions, and I can make mine. I'm staying here.'

'Alick, wait—'

But he had already disappeared. Oran called his name two, three times, but he didn't return. Dugald looked guilty, as if he thought this was all his fault.

'Don't worry,' said Oran. 'He'll come around.'

But she wasn't sure about that. She hung his ashes on a hook on the back of the cabin door and went back on deck with a heavy heart.

Once the boat was ready and lowered into the water, she collected the whalebone cithara and went to the top of the rope ladder. She took her weight on her one good arm and climbed slowly and awkwardly into the boat. She helped Dugald in after her, and waved to the Opera. The captain raised a hand in farewell. Her face was grim.

The crossing was more difficult than Oran had envisaged. At first she sat in the prow with the whalebone cithara, while the Duke rowed them. She directed him as best she could through the reefs and submerged rocks, but he was not a skilled oarsman. In the end they took one oar each, she left and he right. They zigzagged wildly over the waves until she began to thump the bottom of the boat with her heel and sing to keep them in time.

Sunfish, starfish, wispfish, whale,
Whisky, water, ginger ale.

It was a nonsense song that she'd learnt when she was small, a simple rhythm and a simple tune. After two lines, the Duke suddenly joined in.

Shallop, sharpie, schooner, sloop,
Oatcake, cheesecake, lobster soup.

Oran almost let go of her oar. His voice was a beautiful thing. More surprising still was the fact that he knew the song at all. She certainly hadn't taught him.

'Where did you learn that?' she said.

'My maw taught me. When I was a baby.'

'Your *maw*? You mean the Duchess?'

'It was one of the only songs she ever sang to me.'

'But I thought she was tone-deaf.'

He stopped rowing and shook his head. 'She's not. No one has *no* music in them. It only seemed that way if you compared her with Aunt Isla.'

'So she can sing?'

'She used to,' the Duke said. 'I told you, my family have all got a bit of Little Drum in them. Why do you think my maw preserves the instruments in her museum? She could've just made a big bonfire for them. But she didn't.'

Oran considered this, waves slopping over the side of the boat.

'She's not a bad person, my maw,' said Dugald.

'She tried to hang me,' said Oran. 'And she shot me in the hand.'

'She could have shot you somewhere worse.'

'I'd dispute that.'

'She's not bad,' he said again. 'She's just . . .' He sighed. 'Troubled.'

For a second time, Oran found herself thinking of her own mother. 'Running away won't help with that,' she said, almost to herself, feeling the needle of her own guilt.

'I know,' he said. 'But I thought if I found Aunt Isla maybe I could patch things up between them. And I thought if I learnt to play properly, maybe Maw might change her mind about music and singing and every-thing else. I thought I might' – he sniffed hard, and Oran wasn't sure if it he was crying, or if it was just his usual runny nose – 'cheer her up.'

The boat suddenly clattered against a hidden reef, and the pair of them were nearly catapulted into the frothing waves.

'We need to get rowing again,' said Oran, 'or both

our maws will have something else to be troubled about.'

Their tiny boat bucked and veered as the currents became more erratic. Oran struck up the beat with her heel again, checking over her shoulder every other stroke to see how close they were to the rocks. It all would have been much easier if Alick had been with them, but she tried not to think of that.

The pair of them hauled on the oars until they found the slipstream that she knew so well, which seemed to lift them into the air and carry them through the worst of the reef. When they reached the mouth of Bard's cave, Oran hopped out first and did her best to tie them to the usual spire of rock. She kept dropping the rope and losing the end, and before long her bandages were soaked and her hand was stinging from the salt water. Eventually, the Duke flopped out of the boat after her and helped make the knot secure. Oran lugged the whalebone cithara on to her back and waded through the shallows.

They stood at the mouth of the cave, sea spray dripping on their heads, and peered inside. There was a smell of old fish and galleon bird droppings. The cithara was heavy and silent in its bag.

'Is this really where she lives?' said the Duke. He was shivering violently, his jaws like a pair of castanets. She could tell it wasn't just from the cold.

'She's made it quite homely inside,' Oran said, trying to reassure him.

'Why didn't she try to come home?'

'Because your maw sent her here. Into exile.'

'Exile?'

'That's what she said.' Oran paused. 'Although there are so many versions of the story now, I don't know which one to believe.'

'Well then,' Dugald said. 'We'll have to ask her.' He plucked himself up, then sent a sneeze echoing through the cave.

They passed under the arch and into darkness. Oran helped the Duke over the slick layers of flow-stone to where Bard had made her home.

At the top of the slope the fire was lit. Bard was there, silhouetted against its grimy light, sitting in the exact same spot where she had shared a pot of undrinkable tea with Oran and first mentioned the whalebone cithara.

'Caught a cold, have you, my dear?' said Bard. 'If that's the worst of your injuries, I'd say you came off lightly!' She levered herself up and turned to face them. 'And who is this? Your first mate?'

Dugald was looking at Bard with undisguised horror. Aunt Isla must have changed a great deal since he had last seen her. He came forward into the ring of firelight and Oran saw the grin on Bard's face disappear. She and her nephew froze and gazed at each other as if across a wide and impassable ocean.

'Dugald?' She turned back to Oran. 'What is he doing here?'

'He missed you,' she said. 'He thought you were dead. Everyone thinks you're dead.' She waited for a reply and didn't get one. Still the boy stared at his aunt, mute, eyes shining. 'Why didn't you tell me?' Oran said at last.

'Tell you what?' said Bard.

'That you were the Duchess's sister.'

'Because I'm not,' she said, and smiled wistfully. 'Not really. I might have been once. But now I am Bard. The whalebone cithara chose me, Oran, to be its player. And from then on, I became something much greater. I certainly wasn't going to play second fiddle to my tone-deaf sister!' She chuckled, but it echoed coldly around the cave.

'Your sister is coming here,' said Oran.

'Is she now?' said Bard. 'And did you bring me anything else, apart from members of my family?'

Oran nodded. She shrugged the bag containing the whalebone cithara from her shoulders, glad to be free of the burden, and held it out in front of her. The Duke had shrunk back a little.

'What happened to your hand?' said Bard. And then, more sharply: 'Did you try to play it?'

'No!'

'I told you it was not yours to play. No wonder you came away with your fingers burned.'

'But I *didn't* try to play it!'

Bard looked at her askance for a moment, then turned her attention to the instrument. She picked up the whalebone cithara and let the bag fall to the floor. She held its gnarled frame in both hands, caressed the strings, and Oran saw tears roll over her cracked and fissured cheeks.

'You came back to me,' she whispered. 'Of course you did. You found me. Your Bard.'

The Duke finally found his voice. 'Aunt Isla,' he said. 'It's me. It's Dugald.'

She looked at him. 'Hello, Dugald,' she said.

And that was that. She gave the whalebone cithara the embrace she should have given her nephew. He began to sob. Bard didn't notice. She held the instrument to her breast as if it was a babe in arms, and then, ignoring the other two, slowly made her way to the mouth of the cave.

'Where are you going?' said Oran.

'To wait for my sister,' said Bard, and hobbled down to face the roar of the sea.

➤25◄

'What's wrong with her?' said Dugald, trying to compose himself with long and shuddering sniffs.

'I don't know,' said Oran. 'She wasn't like this before.'

Or was she? Bard had always been strange, only now it was unsettling rather than charming. Perhaps Oran had only seen what she wanted to see, heard what she wanted to hear. Perhaps she hadn't listened carefully enough to what Bard was really saying. She was sure Alick would agree with that.

They went to the entrance of the cave and found that Bard was already climbing the Bad Steps. Further out, the *Overture* was still bobbing on the restless swell. Oran could see the members of the Opera lining the sides, and the captain with her telescope. Behind them, the red sails of the Duchess's flagship were already in view. She was closer than they'd thought, bearing down upon them with all the fury of a mother who has had her child snatched from her.

She shouted for Bard again, again received no reply.

'I'm going after her,' she said to the Duke. 'Don't try to follow me. It's dangerous. Stay here in the cave.'

'On my own?'

'It's quite safe.'

'What shall I do if my maw comes here?'

'Keep her in the cave too. I'll try and get Bard – I mean, your aunt – to come down.'

'Why does she call herself Bard? Why doesn't she think she's my aunt any more?'

'I don't know. I'm going to find out.' Oran gave his hand a reassuring squeeze. It was limp as a fish. 'I'll be back.'

She approached the first of the colossal stone steps and began to climb. The going was slow with her injured hand, and her bandages were soon brown and damp from the moss and the algae. She had to lever her body up with her elbows, and once she was on top of one of the steps it was hard to steady herself with only one arm. She hardly kept pace with Bard, even though she was both younger and taller.

The top of Tusk was no bigger than the deck of the *Overture* but surprisingly flat, tufted with dark, coarse grass and violet wild flowers. When Oran finally scrambled up the last of the Bad Steps, Bard was standing in the middle of the clearing staring eastwards. The wind was cold and wild and grasping.

'I wish you hadn't led her here,' she said, without turning around. She was watching the Duchess's ship, sails like embers, approaching the *Overture*.

'I didn't mean to,' said Oran. 'She followed her son.'

'I would have preferred a more sizeable audience. A bit more of a stage. Not to worry. I suppose she's the only audience I need. The only one that still needs convincing.'

'Convincing of what?'

'That I should be the one to rule instead of her.'

'To rule?'

'The cithara chose *me*, Oran. The Chorus chose me, to be the heir of the first players.'

Oran's pulse thumped in her ears, loudly and without rhythm. The feeling of betrayal yawned deeply inside her. It was like a trapdoor had been opened in the pit of her stomach, and her heart had fallen straight through it, taking all of her affection and her goodwill and her trust along with it.

'That was why you brought me to Tusk in the first place, wasn't it? You just wanted someone to find the cithara for you. Someone gullible enough to believe you, and your stories.'

'You brought yourself to Tusk, Oran. You heard my music. You heard the cithara, singing through me. And you knew it was the right thing to do.'

Reeled in like a fish on a line, Oran thought.

'You *used* me,' she said.

'You were the one who suggested going to the Headland, my dear,' said Bard.

'I thought you wanted to help the island. If I'd known this was all just to satisfy your ego—'

And then, suddenly, she heard the echo of Alick's words, from when they'd argued on the Headland. Only then did she understand him properly. Only then did she realize how similar she and Bard were. She'd let the sunlight in on the dark and ugly truth that lay at the bottom of her, and she knew that Alick had been right all along.

'I am helping your island,' said Bard. 'I am liberating you from the Duchess. That's what you wanted all along, isn't it?'

'I just wanted to change her mind.'

'All will change,' said Bard simply. 'My sister's mind

included.' She peered over the edge of the cliff. 'Ah,' she said. 'Here she comes now.'

The Duchess's flagship had dropped anchor next to the *Overture*. It dwarfed the Opera's vessel: a massive, glittering, floating palace. The Duchess's guards had gone aboard and taken control of the other ship, and the captain and her crew were huddled on the deck. The Duchess, however, was not with them. She was being rowed, slowly, erratically, to the base of Tusk.

They waited. Bard closed her eyes, as if she was lost in a symphony of her own making.

The Duchess's arrival was heralded by grunts and curses as she hauled herself up the Bad Steps. Oran saw a slender white hand grasp at the tussocks on the top of the island, followed by another, followed by her grimly determined face. She was still wearing all black, but the lace and silk were stained with salt water and smeared with the galleon birds' droppings. When she pulled herself up on to the plateau Oran could see the sinews stand out in her forearms. She was stronger and bolder than she looked. Rather like her son.

'Hello, Samhair,' said Bard. 'Very kind of you to pay your sister a visit.'

'Where is he?' said the Duchess, her chest heaving. 'What have you done with him?'

'I don't think I know who you mean.'

'My *son*, Isla. What have you done with him?'

'He's safe,' said Oran.

'Be quiet, girl,' said the Duchess. 'She has played you like any other instrument.'

That much was true, Oran thought. She stood perfectly still, mute with confusion. Where did her allegiances lie now? With the Duchess? With neither of them?

The Duchess addressed her sister now. 'You had to finish what you started, didn't you?' she said. She spoke quietly but her words carried far, even amidst the competing winds. 'Not content with destroying the rest of our family, you had to come after my son. Make sure that I am truly alone, and then make your triumphant return to the Headland. "Look!" you'll say. "Even the Duke prefers me to his own mother!" And you'll lead my people in a song and a dance while Samhair, deaf as a post, crawls away into a quiet corner.' Her voice trembled. She hurriedly wiped one eye with her sleeve.

Bard shrugged. 'If you know that your people would rather be ruled by me than you, then why don't you give them what they want?'

Again Bard seemed so familiar to Oran, and yet so completely alien. She had the same plain, straightforward way of speaking that she always had. Before, that directness had sounded like deep wisdom. Now it just sounded unimaginably callous.

'Because it is all trickery! You'll trick them into loving you! Like you have tricked my son. Like you have tricked this girl, who would have been hanged on your behalf.' The Duchess shot Oran a look. 'And who may yet be hanged.'

Oran swallowed. Her fingers went involuntarily to her throat.

'There is no trickery involved, sister,' said Bard. 'Only music. But there is no music in you, so how could you possibly understand?'

'That's not true,' said Oran.

They both turned to her.

'There is music in her,' she said. 'Dugald remembers the lullabies she used to sing.'

Bard snorted. 'Lullabies.'

'I don't know what truer music there is,' said Oran. She remembered another of the captain's pronouncements: *the simplest songs contain the most hidden riches.*

'I am speaking of the great music,' Bard said. 'The Old Music. The music of the sea, and sky, and the earth. Music of creation, and destruction.'

'Destruction, yes,' said the Duchess darkly. 'I remember that much. I remember you driving our ship on to the rocks, and drowning nearly everyone on board.'

Bard wasn't listening. She looked lovingly at the whalebone cithara and began whispering to its strings again. She turned and wandered towards the very highest point of the island, a rocky outcrop that was raised like a podium from the rest of the plateau.

'You,' the Duchess said. Oran spun round. Was she imagining it, or had the Duchess's expression softened slightly, since Oran had mentioned Dugald's lullaby? 'You were singing that horrid song when I came to your island.'

Oran looked back at her in surprise. This hardly seemed the time to bring up 'The Red Duchess' again.

'I'm sorry,' she said. 'It was just a silly song, I didn't really think it was true.'

'Oh, it's true. You just didn't know who it was about.' She pointed to Bard. 'There's the real Red Duchess. She's the one with blood on her hands.'

Once again, Oran's confusion robbed her of words. Was nothing as she'd thought? When she'd spent so much of her life dreaming of wild adventures, was this all the wider world could offer – lies and deception and selfish feuding? She quivered like a cithara string, tuned too tightly.

'I don't understand,' she said. And then added: 'I *need* to understand.'

They both watched Bard climbing on to her stage, shooing away the galleon birds who had made it their nest. After a moment, the Duchess spoke.

'Ever since we were little girls, Isla was the one who showed the most promise. It was Isla who had all the talent, all the charm. My parents found her a teacher – from your island, no less – the best cithara player they could find. They tried to find one for me too, a piper, but sent him home after only one lesson, because it was obvious that I was no musician. But my sister, she was gifted. People came from far and wide to hear her play. What a shame, they said, that Isla was the youngest. What a shame, that Samhair would be the one to inherit the Duchy, when her sister was so much more appealing.'

Oran looked over at Bard. She had taken up a seat cross-legged and was warming up her fingers.

'She knew,' said the Duchess. 'She knew what people were saying, and she loved it. And then there came a time when her teacher left her, and she began to teach herself. Her music became stranger. She practised madly, obsessively. And I watched as one by one the Headlanders and the courtiers and my family fell under her spell. They fawned on her and followed her like trained animals. They muttered that traditions were not important, that there was no reason why the youngest couldn't be Duchess. But they didn't know they were, all of them, being led on a merry dance. Until my sister led them to their deaths.'

'Dugald said there was a shipwreck . . .'

'Isla's doing. We were returning from Harp, and the wind had dropped. Not the slightest breath, for days. We weren't even sure we would make it home. My sister thought this was a fine opportunity to prove her worth. To show everyone what a powerful Duchess she would make. She said she was able to conjure a favourable wind with song alone.'

Just as she'd said to Oran, when she'd left Tusk. Oran knew what was coming, but she asked anyway: 'What happened?'

'I don't know how she did it. I didn't hear what she sang, because I had started blocking my ears long before that. But she played her instrument. And the wind picked up. And then several more winds picked up. And before I could stop her, we were sailing into a storm.' She shook her head, and it was a long time before she spoke again. 'She lost control. We hit a reef and the ship sank. Only my sister and I survived. And then, to make my loss all the more bitter, I returned to find that everyone blamed *me* for the shipwreck. They thought *I* was the tyrant. That *I* had tried to kill my own family.'

Oran looked at her injured hand, and then at the Duchess again. Such a troubling feeling, to hate and to pity at exactly the same time. She felt that way about Bard too. Pitied the both of them.

'Music is a fearful thing,' said the Duchess. 'And this

Old Music is most fearful of all.'

Bard laughed quietly from atop the rock. 'You know nothing of the Old Music,' she said. 'It is beyond your understanding.'

'I was on that ship, Isla,' said the Duchess. 'I think it is beyond *your* understanding too.'

Bard made a strange barking noise. 'I have been alone on this rock for a year,' she said. 'I have had nothing to do but listen. I have heard every kind of music that the world can play. And now I have the instrument to play it.'

She put her fingers to the strings of the whalebone cithara, and Oran saw what a lonely thing it was to play by oneself, for oneself. Bard looked down, not out, biting her lower lip in concentration.

'Don't you dare, Isla,' said the Duchess.

There was the sound of panting from behind them. The Duke, his face pale and sweat-sheened, struggled up the last of the Bad Steps and flopped into the grass.

'Maw . . .' he said.

'No, my love,' said the Duchess. 'Go back down. It's too dangerous up here.'

'Stay here, Dugald,' said Bard. 'You're just in time for a sing-song.'

And she took a deep breath.

When the music started, it did not come from

Bard. It was the Duchess who was singing, softly, unaccompanied, the same nonsense lullaby that Dugald had sung in the boat.

Sunfish, starfish, wispfish, whale,
Whisky, water, ginger ale . . .

She was not tone-deaf at all. Every note was perfect. Her singing was quiet and simple and unadorned. It reminded Oran of birdsong – unpractised, but needing no practice.

Bard's brow furrowed, like ripples in wet sand. 'Stop that,' she said.

The Duchess did not stop. She came towards her sister, slowly, as if she was a wild animal.

'*Stop!*' cried Bard, and she raised her hand to strike a chord on the cithara.

Before the strings could ring out, the Duchess leapt forward to snatch the instrument from her sister. Bard fell heavily on to the rocks, still gripping the frame in both hands. The Duchess tried to prise it from her fingers, but Bard kicked and wriggled and cried out.

'No! You will *listen* to me!'

The Duchess forced Bard's head to the rocks with the heel of her hand and finally tore the whalebone cithara free from her sister's fingers.

Bard got up and lunged at her, snarling, and caught her in the belly with her shoulder. The Duchess dropped the cithara again. They stumbled, and rolled, and kept rolling, and before Oran or the Duke could move or speak, the two sisters had fallen from the edge of the cliff and disappeared, and the wind snatched their cries from their mouths as they fell.

⇒26⇐

Oran and Dugald stood watching the sea surge against Tusk's jagged sides. Its dark surface was webbed with foam, heaving like some vast creature drawing breath, in and out and in and out. On each inhale the waves crashed against the cliffs with enough force to break a frigate into matchwood; in each exhale they split on the sharp rocks beneath them. Oran couldn't see Bard or the Duchess.

'Maw . . .' said the Duke again, but only very quietly, and to no one in particular. The edge of Tusk was crumbling where the grass had forced its roots into the rock beneath, and he stood a little behind Oran, clutching at her sleeve.

Oran picked up the whalebone cithara in her good hand and held it to her chest. The top of the island was silent now. The galleon birds wheeled overheard and made not a sound. 'We should go back,' she said.

The Duke didn't reply. He just kept a hold on her sleeve. Oran didn't know how long they stared into the raging waves. It seemed like hours before the Duke let her edge away from the cliff and wander slowly, dizzily, to the top of the Bad Steps.

The climb down took even longer than the climb up. Oran had the twin burdens of the cithara and Dugald, who seemed paralysed with shock and had to be lugged down from one step to the next like a sack of potatoes. Oran didn't know what to say to him. There was nothing to say. Nothing to sing, either. What song was there could possibly have made sense of what had just happened?

At the bottom of the steps they found the Duchess's boat; two of her guards still sat at the oars looking bored. They quickly straightened up and their eyes flicked from the Oran to the Duke.

'Your Grace,' one of them said. 'Where is your mother?'

Dugald stared at his shoes.

'The Duchess . . . fell,' said Oran.

'Fell?'

'With her sister.'

'Her *sister*?' The other oarsman looked at them. 'Can't be. Her sister died in the shipwreck. It was the Duchess who—'

And then he realized the Duke was still there, listening.

'Take us around the island,' said Oran, climbing into the boat. 'We might find her—' She stopped herself from adding the word 'body' just in time.

The guards wordlessly levered the boat away from the shoal. They spoke to each other in glances, mouths clamped shut. The four of them made a slow and fruitless circle around Tusk, but found nothing, either in the water or out of it. The Duke slumped in despair. He looked tiny, perched on the seat in his wet and hanging clothes.

Their route back to the Duchess's flagship seemed to take for ever, through humps and troughs in the sea as solid and unyielding as wet sand. When they finally pulled up alongside the hull, Oran and the two rowers helped the Duke out of the boat and up the rope ladder.

The rest of the crew didn't know what to do with either of them. They had obviously seen from the ship what had happened to the Duchess. The deck reared and rolled, as though the loss of the Duchess had set the whole world adrift. Across from them, on the deck of the *Overture*, the Opera looked just as lost themselves.

'Your Grace,' said one of the men who had rowed the boat, bowing slightly before the Duke. 'What would you have us do?'

The Duke sneezed. He looked up, not seeing the man, or the ship or Oran. The last living member of the Magmorran family, and he was no older than she was.

'He's in shock,' said Oran.

The crew looked at each other, and then up at the helmsman, leaning on a wheel that was twice Oran's height. The helmsman shrugged. 'Back to the Court?'

'There's nothing for him at the Court,' said Oran. 'He needs somewhere safe and warm.'

'Then where are we meant to go?'

'Take us home,' she said.

The Harr was over Little Drum, muting the colours and the sounds of the harbour. The fields and forests looked ashen, the fishing boats faded and peeling. The lighthouse's lamp was dead. There was no one to welcome them apart from a handful of Magmalley's people, who seemed agitated that the Duchess's flag-ship should be paying them a visit out of the blue.

As soon as both ships were moored, Oran went straight across to the *Overture*, the whalebone cithara strapped to her back with some old pieces of rigging rope. The Opera seemed to have come to a truce with the Duchess's guards, since nobody knew who was in charge any more. In fact, it seemed more than a truce. Guillam was laughing with one of his captors. Erikah was playing knucklebones with another.

Oran went into the captain's cabin, took Alick's ashes from where she'd hung them on the back of the door and tied them to her waist. She called his name, twice, three times. He did not appear. Still angry with her, still disappointed. The pouch felt like a dead weight on her hip.

Dugald was waiting on the quayside with a handful of the Duchess's guards. He watched her coming with a kind of desperate hope, as if she would bring him good news. But she had none to give.

Word of the Duchess's fate was spreading from the new arrivals to the men who were already on the island. Oran wondered where Lord Magmalley was. Wondered what he would say when he found out what had become of his mistress.

She took the Duke's hand and began the walk up the cliff path to her cottage.

'Hey!' said one of the guards. 'Where are you taking him?'

'Home. He needs food and a bed.'

'He's got a bed on the ship.'

'What? His maw's bed?'

No one replied to that.

At the top of the cliffs overlooking the harbour, Oran stopped to let the Duke catch his breath. He panted quietly. Oran herself wasn't particularly tired – she'd made this journey almost every day of her life – but she found her heart would not be stilled. It was a few moments before she realized that she was scared. A deep fear had taken root somewhere in her. What if she was too late? She hadn't seen or heard a single ghast since she'd arrived, and that included Alick. The sunlight was thin, the trees and the grass shrivelled and brittle. Weeds had forced themselves up between the cobbles of the cliff path. There seemed more flies in the air than there had ever been. Oran tried to count up the days that she had been away. It was no more than eight. It felt like a lifetime.

When Oran reached her cottage the front garden looked sickly and overgrown. She could hear the torcs grunting irritably in the paddock behind the house. She paused on the doorstep, her left hand hovering in front of the door, her right dangling painfully at her side. She pictured her maw opening up from the other side. What would she say to her? To any of them? The thought came to her, in a cold rush, that her running away wasn't something that could be patched up with talk, or food, or song. She had made some breach that couldn't be repaired.

The Greymers' words came back to her unbidden.

For she left her maw
On a silent shore
When her home was sorely oppressed.

She knocked on the door.

There was a rustling from the other side, and the scrape of a chair on the floor, and then silence again. She knocked once more. More rustling, then a groan, followed by slow and unsteady footsteps. It wasn't her maw who opened the door, but Granny. Oran was flooded with relief.

Her grandmother squinted. Her eyes went very small, and then very large. 'Oran?' she said.

'Hullo, Granny,' said Oran.

They pulled each other into a tight embrace. Oran breathed deeply into her Granny's shawl. All of her home was there – the smells of torc-wool, of her da's cooking, of her maw's fiddle resin. And she was so warm! Oran felt, suddenly, as if she had been frozen ever since she'd set sail from Little Drum and was only now thawing out.

'Oran, my love,' said Granny. 'We thought you were gone for good.' Her voice was muffled by Oran's skein.

'Where are Maw and Da?' asked Oran.

Her grandmother stepped back and her face became still and serious. 'At the Great Barrow.'

'The Barrow? Why?'

'Magmalley has learnt that we keep instruments there.' Her voice broke. 'The ghasts have left, and now he wants to raid the shrines.'

The Duke suddenly sneezed.

'And who are you?' asked Granny. She gave Dugald a kindly smile, but Oran could see it took effort. 'A citharist, if I'm not mistaken!' She took his fingers in hers. 'Where have you come from? You sound like you've an awful sniffle.'

The Duke still didn't want to speak.

'This is Dugald,' said Oran, gesturing with her bandaged hand.

Her grandmother gasped. 'Oran, your hand! What on the Four Seas *happened* to you?' She raised herself on tiptoes and squinted. 'What's that on your back?'

Oran loosened the ropes she'd used to tie the whalebone cithara to her shoulders. She slung it round and held it in front of her. A twisted and ugly-looking thing.

'I found it,' she said

And for what? she thought. Was it worth it, after all the grief she had put her family through? After everything Dugald had suffered?

But Granny's face was transformed. She was beaming. She looked twenty years younger. 'Oh, Oran,' she said. 'You wonderful thing.'

⇒27⇐

The sight of her living room brought Oran to a standstill. Her eyes pricked at the sight of things she hadn't even realized she'd missed. Her grandfather's dented brass telescope on the windowsill; her granny's needles and balls of wool; the crack in the floor where her da had once dropped a full stewing pot. Unremarkable things that when arranged together took on a whole new significance; a great symphony composed, as all symphonies are, from just a handful of individual notes.

Her granny came back from the kitchen with hot

torc milk for all three of them. She handed out the steaming mugs slowly and deliberately before she said anything.

'Well?'

Oran was staring at her cithara case. It was where she'd left it, on the mantelpiece. She didn't want to open it. She could well remember what the broken pieces looked like. 'Well, what?' she said.

'How on the Four Seas did you find it?' said Granny.

It took Oran the best part of two hours to recount everything that had happened since they'd set out from her front door, under the stars and the silence, eight nights ago. Only Oran spoke. Dugald studied his hands and shivered and said nothing.

Granny listened carefully to their every word with a strange light in her eyes, glancing periodically at where the whalebone cithara leant against the hearth. Her mug of hot milk sat on the table next to her chair, getting cold. Oran reached the end of their story. The struggle between Bard and the Duchess received scant attention – she hardly wanted to remind Dugald of the details.

It was a long time before Granny said anything.

'What a waste,' she muttered. 'And it's all my fault.'

Oran rested a hand on her grandmother's bony knee. 'What do you mean, Granny? How could it possibly be your fault?'

'The Duchess told you that her sister had a teacher from Little Drum, didn't she?'

'Yes . . .'

'I was her teacher.'

Even Dugald seemed to pay attention to that. He raised his eyes from the surface of his drink. The silence swelled to fill the cottage — that horrid, whining silence that had replaced the ghasts, more a presence than an absence.

'You never told me that.'

'I never told your maw, either. I never told anyone.'

'Why? Just because you taught Bard music doesn't make all of this your fault. The Duchess said that things went wrong when Bard started to teach *herself*.'

'I didn't just teach her. I was the one who gave her the whalebone cithara.'

'You?' said Oran. 'You were the one who stole it from the Great Barrow?'

'I had no choice,' she said. 'Though I have been punished for it ever since.'

'What do you mean you had no choice?'

'Isla — when she was Isla, and not this woman you knew as Bard — became obsessed with the story of the Chorus, and the First Instruments. She was extraordinarily talented, Oran. Almost as talented as you.' She smiled, but it faded quickly. 'She convinced herself that she was one of the singers chosen by the Chorus, that she was the only rightful player of the whalebone cithara. And she told me to steal it for her.'

'And you agreed?' said Oran, incredulous.

'You don't agree or disagree with a command from someone like that. She was the daughter of the Duke and Duchess, and sister of the Duchess-to-be. She told me if I didn't get it for her, she could ruin me and my family. Your maw was pregnant with you at the time, Oran. It was hardly the time for our family to be making enemies in high places. So, yes, I fetched the whalebone cithara for her.'

'And she taught herself to play it?'

'She tried,' said Granny, 'although it sounds as if she never mastered it. How could she? The instrument chooses the player, not the other way around. And besides, her intentions were all wrong, Oran. She was arrogant. A show-off, to be blunt. I tried to tell her as much, but she didn't take kindly to that, and sent me away.'

Oran wondered how many people thought that *she* was a show-off. Alick did, certainly.

'Once she dismissed me,' Granny went on, 'I tried to forget about the whole business and move on. But I couldn't. The moment I took the cithara from the Great Barrow, the Chorus punished me. Or perhaps I was punishing myself. The ghasts wouldn't speak to me. My inspiration quite disappeared. I haven't played or sung a single note since.' She studied the whale-bone cithara again. 'Now you have returned it, perhaps . . .' She seemed afraid to say what she was thinking.

Dugald cleared his throat. 'Did you know my maw?' he said, almost whispering.

Granny turned and gave one of her broad and gentle smiles. 'I did, young man,' he said. 'Only met her a few times. But I thought very highly of her back then. Quiet, she was. A real listener. The opposite of her sister.' She paused and seemed to trawl her memories. 'Yes. I would have liked to teach her too. But the cithara was not her instrument. A piper, I seem to remember. Old Crake gave her a lesson once, I believe – but her parents dismissed him because they thought she showed no promise. It is terrible thing, Dugald, to deny someone the music that is inside them. A crushing, ruinous thing.'

'I would like to learn,' he said.

'And I'm sure Oran would like to teach you,' said Granny.

'If my mother was not allowed to sing, I shall sing for her.'

'That is a lovely idea. Only, I am not sure there is an instrument anywhere on the island. Magmalley has taken the lot. Apart from Oran's, that is.'

Oran laughed flatly. It was a meagre consolation,

she thought, to be able to keep the broken slivers and tangled strings of her cithara.

'Then I will ask him to return them to you,' said Dugald.

'You will?'

He drew himself up in the armchair, and sat proudly, though his face was wan and his voice trembled with sorrow.

'I am the Duke. The Duchy of the Headland and the Near and Far Isles will pass to me. He will have to do what he is told.'

⇒28⇐

They had got as far as the town hall when Oran
saw a group of islanders crossing the square in
front of the Broken Bottle. They were marching
towards the Three Widows, the windmills that marked
the westernmost point of the island. They were loud
and purposeful, though Oran thought there was something erratic about the way they moved. It was as if
they had lost some inner tempo that normally guided
their paces.

She hollered after them, and they turned.

'Sea's teeth!'

'It's Cora's girl!'

'She isn't a ghast, is she? I thought they never found her . . .'

''Course she isn't a ghast, you daftie! She's solid as me and you!'

Oran recognized all of them. Old Crake, the beet farmer; Boyle, her cithara teacher from many years back; Maura, who made and maintained the bells in the town hall. All of them not much younger than her granny. Her parents were not among them.

'Hullo,' she said. 'Have you just come from the Barrow?' She nervously put a hand on Alick's ashes.

'Aye,' said Crake. 'We were too late.'

'Too late?'

'That devil Magmalley has already filched a whole load of instruments from the burial chambers.'

'But we won't stand for it any longer!' said Boyle. 'How'll we ever get the ghasts back if they don't have their instruments?'

'So what are you going to do?' asked Oran.

'We're going to get them back,' said Maura. 'One of the guards told us they'd seen him going to Dunhaidh's Reach with them.'

That was odd, thought Oran. Dunhaidh's Reach was the old harbour. It had long fallen into disrepair, half devoured by the waves of the Endless Sea. No one used it any more.

'Why has he gone there?'

'Turns out he's been *selling* our instruments in secret. Merchants and pirates coming from the Green Sea to buy them off him! Turning them to his own profit right under the Duchess's nose!'

Oran looked at the Duke. His face had a hard, determined look to it, though grief was never far from its surface.

'Where are my parents?' she asked.

'Gone ahead,' said Boyle. 'By the Chorus, they'll be happy to see you.'

They looked at Dugald and frowned, but before they could ask who he was Oran was running ahead to the western coastal path.

The Three Widows emerged from the mist, a trio of giants in billowing white dresses. The story went that the windmills had once been fisherwomen who had tried to guide their husbands home from the clifftop by waving their sails, and had continued to wave them desperately, vainly, for ever after. The ghasts said that there had never been a day when the sails of the Three Widows had not turned in the onshore winds. Today, all of the windmills were completely still.

Oran came to edge of the cliff and looked towards the old harbour, but the Harr was still so dense Oran couldn't see any of the bay below.

'I've never seen a fog like this,' said the Duke.

'Neither have I,' said Oran. 'The Harr doesn't usually cover the whole island. And it isn't usually this thick. Or this quiet.'

'Do you think . . .' said the Duke. 'Do you think it's because of my maw?'

'I don't know,' said Oran. 'But if it is, I'm sure you can put it right.'

But could he? Could anyone? She still hadn't seen or heard any ghasts. Even if they returned the instruments to the Great Barrow, and gave the rest back to the islanders, who was to say the ghasts would come back at all? Would anyone remember the songs, if the ancestors had already gone quiet?

She squeezed Alick's ashes, still unsure whether he was with them or not.

When they came to the bottom of the cliffs there was a crowd gathered on the remains of the old harbour. Three of the four piers had fallen into the sea, and the fourth looked as if it wouldn't survive another storm. Out in the bay was a ship, a three-mast barque, whose hull had an odd tint, as if it were covered in moss or foliage. A ship from the Green Sea, where everything was always growing. At the end of the pier were the silhouettes of two figures who Oran knew very well indeed.

Magmalley was shorter than her mother, even in

his gigantically heeled shoes. Oran's maw was bearing down on him, and her fierce words seemed to split the cold fog in two. He was uncowed. His arms were folded and his face wore a look of faint boredom.

Oran and Dugald pushed through the crowd. There was a lot of excited muttering from the onlookers. Magmalley was laughing now, a high, mocking laugh. Oran's mother seized him by the lapels of his jacket, and there was the sound of pearls popping and hitting the pier's rotten timbers. Oran was overwhelmed with a fierce, protective love, as if mother and daughter had swapped places. She marched to the end of the pier and stood behind the pair of them.

'Hullo, Maw . . .' she said.

They both turned, as if framed in some strange dance with each other. Their mouths fell open.

'Oran!' said one.

'Your Grace!' said the other.

Her mother let go of Magmalley and he nearly tumbled backwards into the sea. She flew at Oran and their roles swung back once more. She gathered up her daughter in her arms and squeezed her like bagpipes, standing on tiptoes to kiss her cheeks. Oran spluttered and wheezed and laughed, and, for a moment at least, the fear in her bones quite evaporated.

'You came back to me,' said her maw, in a strange echo of Bard's words.

'I'm sorry, Maw,' said Oran.

'We're all sorry,' said her maw, and beneath her joy Oran heard a deep sadness. Cora squeezed her daughter again, and Oran rested her chin on the crown of her mother's head.

'Where's Da?'

'He's back at the Barrow still. Guarding it against this monster. If anyone else tries to take the old instruments, they'll get a crack on the head from his ladle!'

Oran laughed, and held her maw closer.

Magmalley was looking past them. His body was at a strange, crooked angle, as if he was trying to be obsequious and superior at the same time. 'Your Grace,' he said to the Duke, 'what are you doing here?'

Dugald parted his dry lips. 'I came to see you, Magmalley.'

'An honour,' said Magmalley, and suddenly he looked nervous. 'And your mother is with you, is she?'

Dugald took a long time to answer. He wavered on his feet, like seaweed in a strong current. Oran wormed her way out of her maw's embrace and stood next to him, fearing he might faint and fall. But he straightened himself up, looked the little man in the face, and did not sneeze once.

'My mother is gone.'

'Gone?' said Magmalley. 'Gone where?'

Dugald stared into the murky waters of the old harbour. 'Gone,' he repeated. 'An accident on the way here. That's why I've come to see you.'

'This is a tragedy, Your Grace.' said Magmalley. 'Terrible, grievous news.' He paused, but only for the briefest of moments. 'We must speak in private, so I can bring you up to speed with the legislation your mother had in mind. It is rather complicated. Perhaps' – was that a slight smile at the corners of his mouth? – 'it would be better if someone were to rule in your stead until you are old enough to understand.'

Oran gritted her teeth. It was exactly the same patronizing tone he'd taken with her when he'd come to take her instrument.

'No,' said Dugald. 'I am the Duke. I understand my mother better than anyone. I know, for example, that she wished for all confiscated instruments to be returned to the Headland.' He nodded at the green ship. 'And I know that, contrary to what she wanted, you've been selling them.'

Magmalley swallowed. 'For the good of the treasury, Your Grace.'

'For the good of your own pockets!' said Oran,

unable to control herself.

'I would like the instruments to be returned,' said the Duke.

The crowd on the harbour murmured, just within earshot. Oran's maw made a strange squeak.

'Returned?' said Magmalley. His face contorted. He obviously wasn't used to being told what to do by children.

'They are the property of the Duchy. Which means that they are *my* property. And I want you to give them back. All of them.'

'That may be difficult,' said Magmalley. 'They have already changed hands.'

They looked at the ship from the Green Sea. It was nearly on the horizon. Oran had an idea.

'That won't be a problem,' she said with a smile.

⇒29⇐

For the first time since she'd known them, Oran was glad that the Opera were, indeed, pirates. It filled her with a kind of guilty excitement to watch them go roaring into the open sea and chase down the green ship like a hawk hunting a dove. She could hear the crack of the cannons from where she stood beneath the Three Widows, and thought she caught the captain's laughter on the wind. They took Magmalley with them, along with all the money he had received for the stolen instruments, and for perhaps the first time in the history of the Four Seas a gang of pirates was seen handing gold *back* to the ship they had captured.

With evening falling, the whole island came down to the harbour to await the return of their instruments. The *Overture* pulled alongside the quay with a great, triumphant fanfare. Guillam launched some quite unnecessary fireworks, and sent the seagulls flapping and squawking in terror.

A dozen huge wooden crates were unloaded from the hold and set down among the piles of fishing nets. The islanders gathered to see them opened. Oran was at the front of the crush, along with her maw, and Dugald, and the two mayors. The husband prised the lids off the boxes with an iron bar, while his wife held a lamp in the gloom. They peered inside.

There were gasps of joy. The islanders' instruments, the ghasts' instruments – they were all there, out of tune, but intact. Oran helped to carefully return them to their owners. The mayor took his bombard in his hands, cheeks wet with tears, and climbed on top of one of the pier's mooring posts. The islanders cheered. He raised the mouthpiece to his lips once, twice. Then he frowned. His arms dropped by his sides. The crowd fell silent.

'I can't . . .' he said. 'I can't remember what to do.'

He wasn't the only one. Old Crake was examining his reed pipe as if it was an ancient artefact, something from another sea altogether. Others were blowing into their bagpipes and plucking their fiddles and making a cacophony of squeals and scratches. Oran's maw turned her tuning pegs at random, until one of its strings snapped. It was too much for Oran to bear. She left the crowd and perched on a fishing boat that had been hauled out of the water for careening. She wasn't sure what was worse – having no birth instrument, or having an instrument and not knowing how to play it. There was the whalebone cithara, of course, which was back at the cottage under Granny's watchful eyes. But she'd never play that. Not after everything she'd seen and heard.

Dugald slipped away to join her. He sat beside her on the upturned hull, half scoured of barnacles.

'I don't understand,' he said quietly. 'Are these not the right ones? Did I do something wrong?'

'Not at all,' said Oran.

'Why aren't they making any music?'

'Because we're too late.'

'What do you mean?'

'The ghasts have all gone. No ghasts, no songs.'

'We've not *all* gone,' said someone else.

Oran suddenly felt the pouch of Alick's ashes grow warm, and it was as if a third person was sitting there on the boat with them, hip pressed against hers.

'Alick!' she cried.

And there he was, knees tucked under his chin, gazing at the sad, tuneless scene. Seeing his cold silvery light again was like watching the moon come up.

'Hello,' he said.

'Where have you been?'

'In the Great Barrow.'

'And?'

'It's empty. And dark. And quiet.' Abruptly he turned to her and said: 'Where is it?'

Oran frowned. 'Where's what?' she said.

'You know what. The cithara. You kept it, didn't you?'

'It's back at the cottage,' said Oran. 'Granny's looking after it. If you've just come back to tell me not to play it, you're wasting your breath. I don't want to play it. Not now, after everything it's done to Dugald's family. And anyway, in case you've forgotten . . .'

She lifted up her bandaged hand. He looked at it and then went back to watching the crowd on the quayside. Somebody's seahorn made a noise like an injured animal.

Alick sighed and said: 'I'm afraid you have to.'

'Have to what?'

'Play it.'

Oran didn't know what to say.

'There's only one kind of music that can reach the other ghasts now,' said Alick, 'and only one person who can play it.'

'Who?' said Oran, knowing the answer already, but wanting to hear it, at last, from Alick's lips.

'You,' said Alick. 'It's always been you.'

Oran and Dugald had to run to keep up with Alick as he floated along the coastal path. It seemed he was deliberately trying to keep himself out of earshot. Oran had been home to pick up the whalebone cithara, and it hung heavily on her shoulders. She could hear the Duke panting behind her.

By the time they reached the Great Barrow, she was weak with a mixture of confusion and exertion. She hadn't eaten anything since she'd rowed to Tusk that morning. The only thing she had drunk was the mug of hot milk Granny had given her.

Alick disappeared into the black arch of the burial mound. Outside, Oran's father was sound asleep. It was as her maw had said. He was propped up against the stones, feet splayed, a ladle grasped loosely in one hand. His moustache twitched at their approach, but that seemed the extent of his vigilance.

She crept towards where he lay curled up on the threshold. 'Da,' she said, and put a hand on his arm. 'Da, it's me.'

He gurgled something in his sleep.

Alick reappeared. 'Leave him be,' he said. 'We

haven't got much time. The longer the Silence has them, the less chance we have of bringing them back.'

Oran stood up, looked down at her father. Again, that strange feeling that she was the parent, he the child. Then she looked at Alick. 'Can't you just tell me what I'm supposed to be doing?'

'I'll explain once we're down there,' he said. He looked over her shoulder at the Duke. 'Is he coming?'

'Of course I'm coming,' said Dugald. 'I want to put things right.'

'It's dark,' said Alick. 'And dangerous.'

'I'm good with tunnels,' said Dugald.

'It's true,' said Oran.

Alick looked at them both, then shrugged and said to Dugald: 'Fine. But don't touch anything.'

He crossed over the threshold, muttering to himself.

Oran and Dugald followed his pale glow through an endless maze of tunnels and stairs. For every step forward, there were another five or six downwards, until they must have been well below sea level. The air was cold and earthy. The tunnels grew rougher, wider, as if they had been made by no man or woman's hand. Even at this depth Oran could still see the ancestors' urns and instruments balanced on ledges. They were truly ancient. Their designs were crude, the notation of their music unfamiliar.

They went deeper still, until Oran lost all sense of space and time. The earth beneath her feet softened and the rocks arched higher above them, and for the first time since they had entered the Barrow they heard the echoes of their voices. Overhead, thousands of glow-worms glittered across the roof of the Barrow like constellations in the night sky. Alick led them forwards until they reached a cleft in the rocks. He slipped through with ease, and Oran and Dugald followed, with a little more wriggling.

Inside was a great domed cave.

The silence was like nothing Oran had heard before. It was like a living entity down there in the darkness, watchful and purposeful. It stopped her ears and stilled her fingers. It made her afraid to even draw breath, as if any noise would not only break the silence but the island itself.

'The Moot Hall,' said Alick. 'This is where we gather to discuss island matters. Or used to.'

The Duke pressed himself closer to Oran and squeezed her hand, more for his reassurance than hers, she thought. 'What happens now?' he said. His voice was painfully loud.

'I don't know,' Oran said.

Alick traced a route around the edge of the Moot Hall, and where he went Oran could see the carvings of musical notes in the walls. Each one was a life raft on that ocean of silence — as Alick illuminated the note, she heard its length and pitch inside her head, and was reminded that music was possible, even here. It didn't look like normal musical notation, though. She wasn't even sure if notes had been inscribed on the wall, or if their outline had occurred naturally from the cracking and weathering of the rocks. And when Alick passed by, the combination of light and shadow caused the note to waver and change and split into clusters and chords. Above them were the gnarled and barnacled outlines of eight instruments: fiddle, barrow fiddle, seahorn, bombard, reed pipe, bagpipes, bodhrán, handpan. There was a space above her head for a ninth.

'Oran,' said Alick. 'What can you see?'

'Instruments,' she said.

'And?'

'Notes,' she said. 'It's the Old Music.'

'So you can read it?'

'Yes.'

'And Dugald,' he said. 'What about you?'

'I don't see anything,' said the Duke. 'It's just rocks.'

'That figures,' said Alick. He turned back to Oran. 'Do you think you could sing it from the beginning?'

'Maybe,' she said, and frowned. 'I can't see it properly.'

Alick began his circuit of the chamber again,

illuminating the music as he went. She saw and heard the tune as it emerged, note by note, from the darkness – though it was like no tune she had ever heard or played. And then she said, with a laugh of surprise:

'Oh. There isn't a beginning.'

Alick stopped. 'Good,' he said. 'Go on.'

'That's why it's written in a circle. You can start anywhere, and the music will make sense.'

Alick hummed in satisfaction. He seemed to be coaxing answers from her like he was her teacher. And in a way he was, though she had always been a wayward and far from obedient pupil. Oran came to the realization that this place, so dark and strange and ancient, was his home. She'd only ever thought of him as Alick, the fretful nine-year-old boy who had fallen from his parents' fishing boat, but now she saw properly, for the first time, that he was so much more. He was a ghast. He had crossed over and returned. He was wiser than she could possibly understand.

'What is the song?' she asked. 'Do you know it?'

'All the ghasts know it,' he said. 'It isn't just Old Music, Oran. It's the *oldest* music. The First Song. The one song, that contains all other songs.'

There was a different kind of silence in the Moot Hall now: one which replaced the first, full of awe and anticipation.

'What's the First Song?' asked Dugald, the question

hushed and reverent.

'It's what the Chorus sang,' said Oran. 'At the beginning of everything.'

'There should be nine singers,' said Alick. 'And they should all be playing one of the First Instruments.' He paused. 'But I know you're good enough to play it by yourself. And I know you can play that cithara. Even with the wrong hand.'

Oran looked at him askance. 'You've changed your tune. You never wanted me to play it before.'

'I still don't want you to. But we don't have a choice now. And I know you *can* play it. All the ghasts knew. That's why they told me to go with you.'

'They *told* you?'

'When you were determined to sneak out on your own, I went and told them. They couldn't believe it. They thought the whalebone cithara was gone for good. They said I should go with you and make sure you got it back. They knew they would need you to play it at some point.' He paused. 'Come on, Oran, you didn't really think I'd get in a boat with you of my own free will, did you?'

'But if the ghasts thought I was good enough to play it, why did you keep telling me I shouldn't?'

'I told you why,' he said. 'I didn't think you were ready. I thought you were too proud. And I thought . . .' He looked at his feet.

'You thought what? Alick?'

'I thought I'd lose you.'

'Lose me? Why?'

'You know why. Oran, greatest musician on all the Four Seas! Guardian singer of the Far Isles! Player of the whalebone cithara and chosen citharist of the gods! Why would she want to hang around with boring old Alick? Always telling her to *be careful*, and to *listen to her parents*, and to *stop being so full of herself.* Think about it. It just wouldn't work.'

Oran felt her eyes prickle. 'Then I'll leave it here,' she said.

'What do you mean?' said Alick.

'I'll play what I need to play, then I'll forget all about it. I promise. If it's a choice between the whalebone cithara and you, then I know which one I'd rather give up.'

She didn't need Alick to show her the notes again. The First Song was already in her head, fully formed, going around and around. Had always been in her head somehow. Within it she heard snatches of what Bard had sung to the egg; of what she herself had sung for Magmalley's men, and for the Greymers. She heard Dugald's lullaby, and the dances of the Broken Bottle. She didn't know where one song ended and the other began. They were all the same intricate tapestry.

She took the whalebone cithara in the crook of her right arm and put her left hand – her wrong hand – to the strings. She would have to listen hard. She would have to play slowly and carefully.

'I think,' she said, 'it goes like this.'

And she began to sing.

When Oran plucked the first note in the darkness, it was like sunrise. The song came from her lips of its own accord. Harmony and melody were completely new, and yet had existed for ever. It was not music about the world, but the music *of* the world. A *true* song. All of Little Drum was in it – the sound of the meadows and forests, the silent cliffs and the roaring seas, the sound of fishing and weaving and baking bread, the sound of her ancestors long gone and her descendants yet to come. It did more than describe them; it was, as Bard had once said, the very essence of them. It was neither sad nor joyful, and yet it seemed to contain all the sadness and joy that there was in the world. It sounded like life itself. It sounded like being alive.

A brightness entered the chamber, glinting off the rough and ancient shapes of the First Instruments. Figures appeared beside and above her, blank at first, and then more distinct, like islands revealed at low tide. Ovals of light that looked back at her in astonishment. Parents and grandparents and uncles and aunts, generations stretching back for years beyond Oran's reckoning.

And then the ghasts were singing with her, like a thousand crashing bells, and though she was deep, deep underground Oran knew that the fog over the island was gone, and the moon was shining clearly, and the music of Little Drum was returning to its people as if from a half-remembered dream.

⋙30⋘

O ran flew out of the Great Barrow and into her father's arms. The islanders were coming up the path from the harbour, and the ghasts were streaming from the arch, and there was good deal of bowing and laughing and singing between them. Under the moon they clapped and stamped and the shining earth itself was as good an instrument as any.

'Was this your doing?' said her da, still refusing to release her from his bear-hug.

She tried to speak but spluttered and laughed as the bristles of his beard tickled her face. She inhaled the oily, leathery smell of his sealskin coat.

'I knew it!' he said. 'I knew you'd do it! You brave and talented and clever and daft girl!'

'It wasn't just me,' she said. 'Alick helped. And Dugald. And the Opera.'

'Ah, good lads, good lads, both of you!' He bowed low to Alick and shook the Duke's hand so hard the boy's teeth rattled. 'But what about the Duchess?' he said. 'Where's Magmalley? Why aren't the Headlanders doing anything?'

The Duchess's men had followed the islanders up from the harbour. They stood a little apart in their red and black skeins and pantaloons. They were singing too, but quietly, as if the sound might do them harm.

'Magmalley's still locked up in the Opera's boat, I think,' said Oran. 'And the Duchess . . .' She looked at Dugald. 'We don't need to worry about the Duchess,' she said.

'Aha!' Her da clapped his hands like a pair of cymbals. 'Backed down, did she? That'll show her! The miserable old fruit!'

Dugald let out a little groan.

'Da . . .' said Oran.

'What? Do you have any idea what it's been like while you've been gone? If she tries again, we'll be ready. The Red Duchess deserves everything that's coming to her.'

'Don't say that, Da!'

'Come on, Oran, you were here. You know what she's like. You know the song better than anyone! *The fount of all the seas' distress*, Oran!'

At that the Duke walked away towards the assembled Headlanders, stooped and sniffing. Oran went after him, throwing her da an unimpressed look over her shoulder.

'Dugald, come back.'

He shrugged her off.

'He didn't mean it.'

The Duke didn't reply and kept walking. His mother's guards stopped singing and stood to attention when they saw him coming.

'I would like to go back to the ship, please,' he said to them.

'Don't go to the ship, Dugald,' said Oran. 'You can stay with me.'

'I would rather return to my quarters. I would like to be alone.'

'Dugald . . .'

'It's *Your Grace*,' said one of the guards, planting himself between Oran and the Duke.

'I'm sorry, my da just says things sometimes . . .'

But he began to walk back down the hill with the other Headlanders, surrounded by a halo of blubber lamps. Oran watched the group disappear into the woodland at the foot of the Great Barrow.

Her father came and stood at one shoulder. Alick hovered behind the other.

'Where's he off to, then?' her da said.

Oran didn't reply, wondering whether she should go after the Duke.

'He's not an islander, is he? Don't think I've seen him before.'

Oran sighed and told as brief a version of the story as she could. It was hard when everyone around her was singing and dancing, and all she wanted to do was join in. She would have to compose a song of the whole thing, one day. Just *telling* the tale hardly did it justice.

Her da was confused, and understandably so. 'So it really was the whalebone cithara, then?'

She nodded.

'*The* whalebone cithara? You're sure?'

'Dead sure.'

'And you played it? In the Barrow?'

'I did, Da.'

'Then where is it now?'

Oran just stared at her fingers. It was a good question. How was she ever going to compose any kind of song now, let alone one that did justice to everything she had just been through?

Alick answered for her. 'She gave it back.'

'Gave it back?'

'To the Chorus. To be with its fellow instruments.' There was something in the tone of Alick's voice that made Oran feel a little better. Some of the worry had gone from it. He sounded reassured, somehow. Happier.

'Oh,' said her da. 'Well. Good on you, girl.' He chewed one tip of his moustache. 'Still, bit of a shame. Could have come in handy, couldn't it?'

'I had to, Da,' said Oran.

'Yes, course you did. No good leaving the ancestors without the complete set, I suppose.'

'It's not just that,' she said.

And then, as if to explain the matter for her, she saw something at the bottom of the hill. Where Dugald and the Headlanders had disappeared, another two figures emerged slowly and unsteadily from the trees. Her da saw them too.

'Is that . . . ?' He didn't finish his thought.

Oran saw her maw and granny coming towards them, swaying slightly, as though they had already begun a gentle dance with each other. And for the first time in her life, Oran heard her granny singing.

There followed three days of fine, unbroken weather. The ghasts gathered in flocks, like seabirds, in the streets and the harbours and the houses. The islanders remembered not just how to sing, but where to fish, and when to sail, and how to mend their nets. Voices rang out all over Little Drum, and Granny's was one of the loudest. In fourteen years it hadn't weakened at all; rather, it had mellowed like a fine whisky. Long after the sun had gone down, Oran could hear her humming to herself in her bedroom.

Every day, Oran and Alick went down to the harbour to see the Duke. The Duchess's flagship sat by the quayside, colossal, immovable. It was hard to imagine it ever having sailed at all. Oran called Dugald's name until the guards asked her to leave. He never even appeared on deck. But the ship didn't leave, either.

There were other things to occupy her. She carved a new urn for Alick's ashes, and returned to the Great Barrow with her parents to place it in his family shrine and sing his hearth song. The Opera demanded that Oran and Alick give them a tour of the island, and they obliged, despite the sidelong looks from most of the islanders. Guillam and her da seemed to become instant friends, and Oran frequently came home to find them playing cards or drinking or collaborating on a new recipe together – her da doing most of the cooking, and Guillam most of the eating. Her maw also wasted no time in getting Oran back to her usual tasks. There were torcs to feed, fish to be gutted, potatoes to be scrubbed.

But while life seemed to have returned, there was a hollow silence at the heart of all of it. She was now the only islander who didn't have an instrument. Her maw and da had talked of finding her a luthier and fashioning a new cithara for her, but that didn't make her feel any better. What good was a birth instrument if you hadn't had it since birth? It would take years to get to know each other. It would be like suddenly being given a new set of parents. For all the joy and relief of Little Drum, she couldn't stop thinking about it. A quiet melancholy followed her around from the moment she woke to the moment she went to sleep.

On the third day, she and Alick were walking the beach just south of the harbour looking for mussels. The sand was as fine and white as her Da's bread flour, criss-crossed with the tracks of spindlebills. They sat for a moment to soak up the sun. Oran was watching a tiny fishing boat moving laboriously across the horizon when Alick said suddenly:

'The ghasts are talking about you.'

'They are?'

'They haven't spoken about anything else since they came back.'

'Oh.' Oran dug her fingers into the hot sand. 'What are they saying about me?'

'I'm not sure I want to tell you. It'll be no good for your ego.'

'I don't feel like I have much of an ego at the moment.'

'Well,' he said. 'They think very highly of you. You're not supposed to be able to play the Old Music, you know that? No one has played it for thousands of years.'

She shrugged.

'They say you're a very special kind of musician. A special kind of listener.'

She looked back at the horizon, found the fishing boat had hardly moved. It wasn't under sail. Someone was rowing it – a strange thing, so far out to sea.

'Looks like that's all I'll be, doesn't it?' she said.

'What?'

'A listener.' She flexed her injured hand. It was starting to heal, but she still couldn't move three of her five fingers, and the wound smelled funny no matter how much she washed it. 'I miss my cithara,' she said, and her eyes were suddenly hot with tears. 'I miss it so much.'

A group of spindlebills suddenly took to the air in a clatter of wings and a chorus of tweeting. Oran turned to see the Duke, washed and rested and finely dressed, accompanied by two Headlanders. She sniffed and wiped her eyes, embarrassed.

'Dugald . . .'

'Hello.' He raised a gloved hand in an awkward wave.

'Where have you been? We've been trying to talk to you for three days!'

'I was in my cabin,' he said. 'Practising.'

'Practising?' Just the word, the thought of it, nearly brought the tears back again.

'I sent my men to the Five Fingers to fetch me a cithara of my own.'

'Oh,' said Oran, swallowing back her envy. 'That's nice.'

'I've been writing a song,' he said. 'About my maw.'

Oran and Alick looked at each other.

'I thought,' the Duke continued, 'if it was a song that spread all the lies about her, I could sing something new to tell the truth.' He paused. 'It's sort of her hearth song, I suppose.'

Oran smiled sadly. 'I think that's wonderful, Dugald.'

'I don't know if it is,' he said. 'But I need people to hear it. If people are going to know the truth about my maw, I'll have to sing it in public. So ...' He paused and squinted against the sun. 'Could you organize a dance?'

Oran didn't reply at first. She listened to the birds, and the breaking of the waves. She looked at the rowboat, still barely moving, then back at Dugald. His eyes had a kind of desperate, fearful hope in them.

'Of course I can,' she said at last.

'I'll tell the ghasts,' said Alick.

'Oh,' said Dugald, as if he hadn't considered that. 'Thank you.'

He and Oran smiled weakly at each other, as if they had just agreed to go through with something that neither of them really wanted. The Duke was very nervous, no doubt. But for Oran, the thought of attending a dance without an instrument to play filled her with a feeling that was not unlike dread.

❧31❧

The mood in the Broken Bottle was one of wild, joyous abandon. It was the first dance since the Duchess's fateful visit, and the tavern had been filling with musicians from all over the island since midday. They had also been joined by the Opera, who were happy to accompany them on their guitars and accordions and brass horns, and happier still to add new songs to their repertoire. They also had a new member in the form of Lord Magmalley. He was tied to a chair, without his earplugs, in the middle of the horn section.

No one had yet taken to the stage, though there had been several impromptu performances of 'The Sea Cow's Daughter', 'Deep Dark Damp' and 'The Lay of the Lobster Pot'. Oran was sat at a table at the front of the room. Next to her were Alick and Dugald. The latter was paler than she'd ever seen him and shuddering with nerves. Opposite her – though they were rarely actually in their seats – were her maw and da. A space had been cleared in the middle of the tavern, and her parents had been spinning and leaping and laughing for most of the evening, only returning, red and sweating, to gulp down a few mouthfuls of water or ale before plunging back into the dance.

Granny wasn't anywhere. Not at the table, not with the dancers. In fact, Oran hadn't seen her since the previous afternoon.

She scanned the tavern and saw Guillam come swaggering over, his belly straining his shirt like a wineskin, singing loudly to himself:

Johnny-o fell in a lobster pot,
He got himself stuck, and that was his lot;
He lived in the pot day in and day out,
And he couldn't stand up and he couldn't turn about.

He slumped on to a stool.

'Why so coy, Oran?' he said. 'I know you're dying

to play. You can borrow a guitar again, if you fancy. What about the one you played for the Greymers?'

Her mother whirled around in her chair. 'The Greymers? You saw them?'

'Ach, pish. He's from the Opera, Maw,' said Oran. 'You can't believe all his tall tales.'

Oran's account of her journey to the Headland had been judiciously filleted when she'd told it to her mother. She didn't want to give her any unnecessary worry, even if it was after the event. The Greymers, the whelks, the hanging – she'd omitted all of it.

'Well?' said Guillam.

'Well, what?'

'Are you going to play something?'

She shook her head. 'I don't want to borrow someone else's instrument. I played for the Greymers because I had to. Here . . .' She sighed. 'It doesn't feel right.'

'So you *did* play for the Greymers?' her maw intercepted.

Oran tried to change the subject – from the Greymers, from the aching lack of her cithara. 'The Duke's going to play something though,' she said.

Dugald's eyes went as wide as a wispfish's. She rested a hand on his knee. He was shaking. 'Am I?' he said.

'Aren't you?' she replied.

The Duke looked around the table, then took a deep, tremulous breath, and nodded.

They waited for the current dance to end. The islanders all got to their feet when they saw Oran taking to the stage and began clapping and hooting. The ghasts gave out their golden glow, and the very timbers of the Broken Bottle seemed to bow and creak with the warmth of her reception. She went to the rear of the stage and fetched a wooden stool for the Duke, then beckoned him to join her. The applause died down suddenly when it became clear that Oran was not going to be the one singing.

Dugald crept up the steps after her. The islanders hushed each other, curious to hear what their new lord and master had to say for himself. From the audience's point of view, thought Oran, it must have looked very similar to the night when the Duchess had first arrived to make her pronouncement. There was the squeaking of the landlord polishing a glass with a cloth, and then even this faded away.

Oran left the stage. The Duke cleared his throat.

'I am no musician,' he said. 'And I have no birth instrument, save my voice, so . . .' He trailed off.

The islanders leant in to listen. He looked down at Oran. She tried to give him a reassuring smile.

'I am sorry, for what my mother did,' he said. He took several breaths. 'And I understand if you cannot forgive her. But I would like you to know more about her, and then perhaps you'll understand why she did the things she did. She was not a bad person, my maw. But—' He seemed lost for words. He glanced up at the roof and Oran thought he might burst into tears. But he set his jaw, and looked out over the audience, and said: 'Well, the song will say it better than I can.'

He unstrapped the cithara case from his back and took up his seat on the stool. Once he'd taken the instrument out it took him an age to get it in tune. It was a very simple cithara, three-quarter size, it looked like. Still he fiddled with the tuning pegs. The islanders began to get restless. Oran chewed the inside of her cheeks with worry.

Dugald began the first verse without even looking up.

Listen and I'll tell you true
Of two Duchesses, red and blue;
Sisters from themselves estranged,
Both by bitter feuding changed.

There were intakes of breath from the audience. They were obviously surprised by the quality of his singing. Dugald was halfway through when Oran saw that the door to the Broken Bottle had swung open. Some of the islanders turned in their seats; others were captivated by the Duke's song.

Hear how this one, blind with pride,
All the ancient laws defied;
Hear how this one, racked with fear,
Made song and sister disappear.

He still hadn't noticed the newcomer. Oran looked towards the open door, holding her breath. A lone figure stood on the threshold, dripping. A woman, in a dress or a robe of some kind. Her hair was unbound, wreathed with seaweed. She did not come any further forward. She cocked her head slightly, as if also listening to the song. Dugald had not stopped singing. His eyes were closed, and his voice was pure as spring water.

Know this grievous, woeful rift.
Cast my mother's mind adrift . . .

'That tune,' said the figure at the door. 'I know that tune.'

The colour of the ghasts changed instantly. Alick appeared next to Oran's ear.

'It's her,' he said. 'It's—'

'I know,' said Oran.

The Duchess staggered into the tavern, barely able to stand. She steadied herself on one of the tables, and it gave way beneath her. She fell to the floor. The Duke finally looked up.

The rest of the islanders looked at the Duchess's long, thin body, her limbs sprawled over the floor like pieces of flotsam. They seemed reluctant to help the woman who had brought so much anguish to Little Drum.

Dugald jumped down from the stage and pushed his way through them. Oran followed. He knelt by his mother and cradled her head in his lap. 'What are you all waiting for?' he said, looking frantically at the crowd that had gathered. 'Get her some water! And give her some room to breathe!'

It was Oran's own mother who came back from the bar with a tankard and poured a few drops between the Duchess's cracked lips. Oran looked her over. She was a pitiful thing. She was still wearing that slim, plain dress of mourning. Her hands were blistered and bleeding. Her face was gaunt and etched with grief. There was no performance now, no mask, and Oran thought she could read in those lines the loss of her parents, her husband, and now her sister.

An hour passed before she felt strong enough to speak again. She ate a little dry bread, drank more water, then some whisky to fortify her spirits. Dugald propped her up next to a table. From the corner of the room, tied to his own chair, Magmalley was calling to her. She ignored him, and his voice grew hoarse and then silent.

'What happened, Maw?' said Dugald.

The Duchess licked her lips and hissed quietly in pain. 'The waves took me under,' she said. 'There are blow holes, under the island. I got sucked down. Back into the cave.'

'What about your sister?' said Oran.

The Duchess looked at her, and there was a flash of the cold, blue flame, but it dwindled quickly.

She just shook her head.

'But how did you get back here?' her son asked.

'You left your rowboat,' she said to Oran.

And Oran remembered, suddenly, the tiny silhouette she'd seen crawling across the horizon earlier that afternoon.

'Maw,' said the Duke. 'While you were gone, I . . . I thought . . .'

'You thought you'd return their instruments. I saw.' She paused. 'I heard.'

The Broken Bottle went quiet again.

'That song,' she said. 'I used to sing it to you when you were a baby. I remember the tune. Although the words were different.'

'I gave it new words,' said Dugald.

'Yes. I heard that too,' said the Duchess. 'About me.'

'I'm sorry,' said Dugald.

'Sorry?' The Duchess looked at him long and hard. Then she blinked and looked down in her lap, as if to hide her tears. Dugald held her.

Oran looked away. This was something, she thought, that didn't deserve an audience. The rest of the islanders began to disperse.

'No,' said the Duchess. 'Don't go anywhere.' Her voice still contained all the authority of someone who had spent a lifetime telling other people what to do. She sneezed all of a sudden – a sneeze as powerful as any that had come from the Duke. The islanders froze. 'You cannot leave the rest of the song unsung. Can you?'

The islanders looked at each other. There were several raised eyebrows. Dugald held his cithara stiffly for a few moments, and then began to pick out the tune again. Then, one by one, the islanders and the Headlanders and the ghasts picked up the threads of the song and joined him, though they did not know the words.

The Duke and the Duchess departed the following day. Oran stood on the harbour with Alick, watching the crew make the flagship ready. Most of the islanders were there too, her maw and her da still bleary from the previous night. The dance had continued almost until dawn, though the Duchess had retired to her quarters soon after Dugald had finished playing his composition. That was when the night had begun in earnest, and a wild night it had been. Oran had enjoyed herself, but her lack of instrument still cast a shadow over her. There was something else too. She was worried about Granny. She'd missed the whole of the dance, and she wasn't at the harbour now.

'Maw says we have to go.'

Oran looked up in surprise. Dugald was standing before her. She'd been completely lost in her thoughts.

'Right-o,' she said. 'How is she?'

'Maw? She's all right. Tired.'

'Do you think she'll—'

'I don't know what she's going to do,' he said quickly. 'But she didn't take your instruments back again, did she?'

'No. That's a good thing.'

'And she's still got Magmalley in handcuffs in the hold.'

Oran laughed. 'Perhaps you'll think of a song to win him over as well?'

Dugald sniffed. 'I think that's optimistic.'

'That's what everyone said about your maw. *Song for winter, song for spring, song for all the tides may bring.*'

'What's that?'

'Something my granny taught me.'

The helmsman called out to them, and Dugald

turned and waved. The Duchess was on the deck, looking out to sea, very still. She was wearing a different dress for the first time since she'd arrived on Little Drum, a loose, velvet gown the colour of deep water. The Blue Duchess. Just like Dugald's song.

'You'll come and visit?' said the Duke.

'I'll try,' said Oran. 'But I don't think I'll convince Alick to join me.'

'I'll come,' said Alick, 'as long as you don't insist on sailing the whole way on an upturned vegetable box like last time.'

The Duke hugged Oran and bowed to Alick. 'Well,' he said. 'Bye then.' Then he wiped his nose on his sleeve and went up the gangplank to join his mother, who was still lost in thought.

'Do you think she's changed?' said Alick. 'I mean, *really* changed?'

'I don't know,' said Oran. 'I hope so. She doesn't need to worry about her sister any more, does she?'

Alick shrugged.

'What's that supposed to mean?' said Oran.

'She didn't *actually* say Bard was dead, did she? And if the Duchess survived . . .'

Before Oran could answer, there was the sound of heavy boots and heavier jewellery on the quayside behind her. The captain was there with the rest of the Opera.

'We're off too,' she said.

'Off?' said Oran, surprised at how upset she was. 'Off where?'

'In whatever direction she's not going.' The captain pointed to the Duchess's flagship, which was drifting like some great beached whale back out into the open sea.

There was more hugging and toasting and painful backslapping, more reassurances that they would all see each other again, more invitations to play together one day. The captain gave Oran her three-pointed hat to keep.

'The true captain of the *Overture*,' she said.

True to their word, they let down the sails and made a course in the exact opposite direction to the Duchess – due west. What audiences they hoped to find in the Endless Sea beyond the Far Isles Oran did not know, but they held steady and were soon out of sight.

Oran kept watching the horizons, east and west, long after both ships had disappeared and the crowd had dispersed. The sky was overcast, the weather unsettled. She listened to the gusting winds and chopping waves and thought, ruefully, that if she'd had the whalebone cithara with her she could have played a snatch of the Old Music to send them on their way – a song to calm the sea, and set a favourable breeze in all of their sails.

Then she heard her maw calling her from the clifftop, and went to feed the torcs, still with half a mind on what Alick had said.

When she got home, her parents were standing by the hearth waiting for her. They wore serious faces. Alick was floating behind them. Granny was there too. All of them looked expectant, as if waiting for Oran to explain herself.

'Granny!' she said, though something about the atmosphere in the room stopped her from running to embrace her. 'Where've you been? You missed the dance.'

Granny looked at Oran's parents. Nobody spoke.

'What?' said Oran. Surely she couldn't be in trouble already? She hoped that saving the island would have given her a free pass for at least a month or so.

Granny took a small step to one side. Alick wafted in the opposite direction. Oran frowned. There, balanced on the mantelpiece, was a cithara.

'You got me a replacement?'

She tried not to sound disappointed. Still nobody spoke. Her Granny smiled and gestured for Oran to pick it up.

She'd only taken one more step towards it before she realized that this was not any cithara. It was her cithara. She knew the lines and curves of it as well as her parents' faces. It was all in one piece now, with new strings and one new tuning peg that was a slightly different shade of white to the others. The places where Magmalley had broken the frame were tiny hairline fractures, only visible under the lacquer if you looked very closely. Its arms shone blue in the hearthlight.

'It's you . . .' she said, and in a rush she swept forward and gathered up the instrument and squeezed it to her chest. It was already warm, humming to be near her again.

It was some time before she was composed enough to say anything. Oran's body was all heart, all laughter and tears. She hugged Granny, and her parents, and tried, as always, to hug Alick.

'I don't understand,' she said, still light and woozy with the hilarity of it all. 'Who fixed it?'

'I did,' said Granny.

'But *how*?'

'Did your parents never tell you I was a luthier myself? I know citharas inside and out. That was why they sent me to teach the Duchess's sister.'

'But it was in pieces!'

'A bit of patience. And a lot of kelp-glue.'

Oran couldn't tell if she was joking or not.

'And some help from the ghasts,' Granny added, when she saw Oran was still frowning. 'It's not just music they inspire.'

Oran ran her long fingers over the arms. Her grandmother had worked wonders.

'Well, come on, girl,' said her maw, beaming, 'we haven't got all day!'

'What do you mean?'

'Tune up, and we'll have a sing-song! The whole family. For the first time since you were born!' She fanned herself with one hand and fell into a chair. 'By the Chorus, I am quite overcome.'

Oran gently turned the pegs until the strings agreed with each other. The cithara purred in her arms. She would have to play with her left hand, but that didn't matter any more. In a strange way, she was looking forward to learning everything all over again. It just meant she got to spend more time with her birth instrument.

Her granny took up her own cithara and her maw raised her fiddle bow. Oran's da clutched his bagpipes under one arm and they wheezed into life.

'All right, all right, settle down,' he said, and gave them an affectionate pat.

Oran looked at the four of them, poised, waiting, listening, grinning. She took her cithara in hand, feeling the slight ridges against her skin where Granny had repaired the damage.

She grinned too, then took a deep breath, and began to play.

⇒CODA⇐

Oran hauled hard on the mainsheet and brought her little boat around to face home. It was late afternoon, but the sea still held on to the warmth of the day. A steady wind filled the sail and she barely needed to touch the tiller. Occasionally she would give it a nudge with the elbow of her right arm, since her good hand was occupied with the rigging. She still hadn't quite got the hang of it.

She'd fought the urge to return to Tusk for nearly a month, not least because she wanted to show her maw that she could do as she was told. But curiosity had got the better of her. She'd left early in the morning in her new boat, the *Urchin's Revenge*, and spent a good three hours exploring the island from top to bottom.

Bard was, indeed, gone. So were all her things. The cooking pots, the sealskin rugs, her makeshift cithara. There was no sign the cave had ever been inhabited. They couldn't have been taken by the tide, because Bard had made sure to build her home far away from the water's reach. The organ continued to play its lonely, endless tune. Oran wondered where Bard might be. Afloat on some makeshift raft? Marooned on another island? Down on the seabed, food for fishes? She hoped the last was not true, though it seemed the most likely. Despite all that had happened, she still felt like she had a lot to thank Bard for.

She was still some way from the harbour when the wind dropped and the *Urchin's Revenge* came to a standstill. The water slapped lazily against the sides. Oran waited to see if the sail would fill of its own accord, and when it didn't, she took her cithara out from under the bench and opened the case. It thrilled in the cold air.

'I know,' Oran said, 'but you'll have to do your bit if we're going to be back in time for dinner.'

She stood in the bows of the boat and listened. It came to her easily these days, the Old Music. She hadn't believed it at first, but then the more she had practised – in secret, always – the more it made sense. Why did it matter if she had the whalebone cithara or not? '*A bad musician always blames her instrument,*' as her maw had always said.

She stood on the very tip of the prow, as steadily as if it had been dry land. She listened to the duet of the sea and the air. It was the same music they had played in the beginning, and the same music they would be playing at the end, when the Long Silence returned to the world and settled over everything.

She put her fingers to the strings of her cithara, and they found the Old Music of their own accord. She was soon lost in the melody. A trio, now – Oran and the wind and the waves. She heard a warm easterly breeze and matched its tune. It came to her, and filled her sail, and guided her towards the harbour like a careful, gentle hand.

Acknowledgements

Biggest thanks go, as ever, to my house band, 'The Chickens': Kesia (lead guitar), Barry and Rachel L (backing vocals), Esther (keys), Jazz (bass), Laura (drums), Sarah (tenor sax), Rachel H (cor anglais), Elinor (theremin). This book would have been a wild and meandering prog-rock monstrosity without all of their support, guidance and good taste. Thanks to my agent Jane Willis, for getting all this going in the first place, and for her counsel and kindness; to Sue Cook, for the final polish; to Olga Baumert for the beautiful cover.

I was incredibly lucky to be able to write bits of this book in some very nice houses in some very nice parts of the world. Thanks to the wonderful, soulful, music-full Sam Johnson, and to Mel, Evie and Arthur for probably my best ever month on planet earth; to Helen and Cal and all the Quails; to Sande and Max; to Sabine and Ulf; to Titus and Carrie; to Struan and Frankie and team Erskine; and above all to my other family – Dave, Mary and Duncan – for taking me in and putting up with me and my cursèd toe for so long.

Finally – headlining the acknowledgements stage for the second year running – thanks to Mr William Dollard, for the encouragement and the critique and the ideas and the laughs and, obviously, the music.